STRUCK

LIGHTNING HOPKINS BOOK 1

KEITH SOARES

CONTENTS

Also from Keith Soares   vii
Newsletter   ix
Preface   xi

PART I
ELECTROMAGICIANS

1. Chasing Thunder   3
2. About EMs and Stickmen   7
3. Mr. Gold Muscle Car   11
4. Economy Class   17
5. AM Radio   21
6. Be It Ever So Humble   27
7. Percival's Dragon   33
8. The Fuse Box   39
9. Sponge   45
10. In the Court of the King   51
11. The Anger Quotient   57
12. Night Boats   63

PART II
STICKMEN

13. In the Name of Science   71
14. Dealing with Regulars   75
15. The Hunt Begins   81
16. Power Sources   87
17. The High Order   93
18. Viva la Revolution   99
19. Intruder   103
20. Come Together   109
21. Nowhere is Safe   113
22. Headlong Flight   119
23. Thieves in the Night   125
24. The Writhing in the Pit   129

PART III
WAR OR PEACE

25. Fugitives   139
26. The Storm Before the Calm Before the Storm   145
27. Asking for Trouble   151
28. Revelations   157
29. Strength in Numbers   161
30. The Anger Quotient, Revisited   167
31. A Friend in Need   173
32. What Is It Good For?   179
33. Changing of the Guard   183
34. The Longest Road   191
35. The More Things Change   197

The End   199
Newsletter   201
About the Author   203

Bufflegoat Books LLC
First print edition March 7, 2020
ISBN 978-1-7342349-2-3
Original publication date December 1, 2018

Cover Photography: Dave Scavone, Scavone Photography
Model: Stephanie Japec
Other images licensed from iStock by Getty Images

Dedicated to the Ohrens, who unwittingly inspired parts of this story.

ALSO FROM KEITH SOARES

The Oasis of Filth

Part 1 - The Oasis of Filth

Part 2 - The Hopeless Pastures

Part 3 - From Blood Reborn

—

The Fingers of the Colossus (Ten Short Stories)

—

John Black

For I Could Lift My Finger and Black Out the Sun

If Only Every Moment Was Black and White

And It Arose From the Deepest Black

The Night Is Black, Without a Moon

On a Black Wind Blows Doom

The Black Eye of the Beholder

In the Black Veins of the Earth

Cloak of Black, Mantle of Sorrow

—

Lightning Hopkins

Struck

Twice

NEWSLETTER

Sign Up for Keith Soares's New Releases Newsletter

Get release news and free books, including private giveaways and preview chapters. To join, just visit KeithSoares.com and select the option at the top of the page to get two free books, or go directly to the newsletter sign up form.

facebook.com/KeithSoaresAuthor
twitter.com/ksoares

PREFACE

Alexandria, Virginia
January 2020

Like many stories, this one began with the question, "What if?"
Specifically, in this case, what if something important happened
when you were very young, and you had no memory of it
whatsoever?

Most adults have little to no recollection of their early childhood, and
what they can remember is often heavily influenced by outside information like photographs, video, or the storytelling of others. We actually tend to recall almost nothing from under age two, and very little
prior to age seven, which is conveniently about when the
hippocampus — the section of our brain responsible for long-term
memory — is basically done with making new neurons.

And that's the interesting part — we're not talking about some soap
opera level of drama where the main character suddenly hits their
head and can't recall a thing, we're talking about a real phenomenon
called "childhood amnesia," and it strikes just about everyone.

So... what if really, really important things happened in your early childhood, and you had no recollection of them? What if you are not the person you thought you were, and those around you aren't the people you thought they were?

Lyn Hopkins is about to find out.

Keith Soares
keith@keithsoares.com

PART I

ELECTROMAGICIANS

1

CHASING THUNDER

Ever been struck by lightning? I have. Like 500 times. So far. At least.

It's weird, you know? It isn't the initial strike — that kinda makes everything numb, like you'd think it would. No, it's the after effects. Personally, I hate what it does to my teeth. Makes them feel strange, almost thick. If you've eaten spinach and felt that odd coating on the enamel of your incisors afterward, you know. It's like that, times a million. There's an acrid smell, too, but I sorta suspect that's my hair frying, so I'd rather not think about it.

But I've got to do it. I've got to have the lightning. Without it, I wouldn't be able to make magic. That's where my power comes from.

Right now, I'm chasing a storm. Well, technically it's a tornado. They can be the best kind. Energy, twisted up, all in one place. This one's a doozy. Well worth the effort. An F5, the strongest kind. Most years, there are only one or two of these bad boys, so I have to get to it first.

An F5, with all of its energy potential, could mean one or two months of charge, depending on how you use it. That's a hell of a lot. Your average single bolt of lightning is only a few days worth. Maybe a week, if you played it pretty cool.

Besides, I love the thrill of diving into a tornado, being swept up by it, probably struck by lightning dozens of times. It's a rush. Twirling around in midair until the storm is done with me.

I don't fear it — why should I? A mere storm can't hurt me.

And when it finally spits me out, when I land in some field in rural Nebraska or wherever the twister takes me, I'm one of the most powerful human beings on Earth.

At least for a while.

But I'm behind. The damn storm shifted, the roads weren't conveniently located, and okay, maybe I woke up 20 minutes later than I intended. Sue me. I stomp on the gas pedal of my rental — an American-made SUV *upgrade*, because, darn it, I'm worth it — and race to catch up with the twister. If the thing dissipates, I'll get a charge, but a weaker one. That would suck. The truck alone is gonna cost me serious cash.

And Percival is on my ass.

So I need to hurry.

An RV passes, going south, probably trying to evade the storm. Pretty much the opposite of what I'm doing.

I slam the wheel left, busting off road. The SUV dives into a ditch, then bounces up, rattling my teeth, making me bite my tongue. There's a coppery taste in my mouth, blood. Not too much, though. Besides, if I succeed, it's worth a little bloodshed. Then I'm in a corn field, racing through it like the chase scene in a freaking movie, husks and stalks flipping over the hood. Pretty sure I just waived my security deposit. Kevin is going to be ticked off — my brother hates when I piss money away. Heedless, I rev the engine. The SUV handles well, but off the pavement it seems like too much of the power just gets gobbled up by the dirt.

I'm plenty familiar with power being gobbled up.

It makes me want to go faster.

There's a black blur, suddenly pulling ahead on my left. "No," I say, pounding the wheel. "How's that possible?"

"Age before beauty, Lyn!" Percival Farimir shouts through the open window of his own SUV. Apparently he got the better model. It might not be shiny and new after he's done with it, but his black monstrosity mows the field like a harvester on steroids.

"That's not how you're supposed to use that phrase!" I yell back. How he hears me — how I hear him — is a tiny mystery. An offshoot of our magic. "And don't call me *Lyn*, farmer boy!"

"Oh, sorry, Lyn! I always forget you want to be called *Lightning*. Especially when I'm the one getting all the charge today!" I see a flash of wavy blond locks, those too-white teeth grinning, those intense-blue eyes sparkling, as the black SUV somehow goes faster, separates. "And *you* shouldn't call me *farmer boy*! I'm from the city, remember? Never been to a farm in my life!" He's getting ahead.

"Damn it," I mutter as I press the gas pedal harder down, even though it's already floored. "Never? You're in a corn field *right now*, farmer boy," I say, but with very little conviction. The distance between us continues to grow. Without warning, a scarecrow with blackened eyes appears directly in front of me and I swerve, just on instinct. The thing looks way too much like a Stickman. I hate Stickmen.

The zig is just enough to cement Percival's lead as his truck reaches the edge of the tornado. I know what he's going to do — I've done it myself, of course — but it still looks completely crazy from my point of view. I may be different than most people, regular people, but I'm not a complete freak. I know a slightly-bad-ass, definitely-insane move when I see one.

Percival opens the driver's door with his SUV still flying and bouncing across the field. He probably dropped a brick on the accel-erator. I've seen him do it before. Hell, *I've* done it before. Just as the vehicle is swept up by the tornado, he jumps. Not away from the storm, but into it. And it takes him up in its swirling, powerful arms, like a welcoming lover.

I slam on the brakes, knowing it's done. Once the storm has a focal point, you can't wrest it away. Percival won. At best, some residual energy of the tornado might hit me as it departs. I watch helplessly as Percival is lifted, arms outstretched like he's having a religious experience. Then the lightning starts to strike, called to him from out of the clouds, the source of his magic — and mine — attracted to him just as he's attracted to it. I catch my own face, frowning in the rearview. "What? Don't look at me like that." Sometimes I talk to myself, I admit. "You could've gotten up earlier this morning, you know?" There's a crashing sound, muffled in the distance, as Percival's black SUV lands probably a quarter-mile away, likely totaled. "Looks like nobody's getting their security deposit back today. As always," I say to the mirror.

I get out and stand in the field for a while, but it's mostly hopeless. I pick up a little residual charge, just from the electricity in the air. It's enough to boost me but not for very long. So I pull out my phone and open it to the weather radar. I have to be careful how I touch the device — or really any device. I use a seriously rubberized case plus I wear those special gloves that actually work on touch screens. I can't touch the thing directly, especially not in moment like this. Not if I want it to keep working. The big, multicolored blob of the F5, Percival still inside, is an angry spot on my screen, moving away from the red pin that screams *You are here! Not where the storm is!*

I pinch the screen with my gloved hand to zoom out. "All right, big boy. You must have a baby sister around here somewhere, right?"

2

ABOUT EMS AND STICKMEN

Lightning Hopkins — that is, *me* — was born, as Percival so unfortunately is aware, Lyn Marianne Hopkins, just a bit more than 23 years ago. I never liked the name Lyn. I *hate* the name Marianne. Hopkins? Meh. It's a name.

And, yeah, being 23 means I usually have to pay the so-called Youth Surcharge to rent a car, like I don't know how to drive or something. I hate that. I'll be thrilled when I hit 25 and that little insult is put to bed. Of course, considering the condition of the SUV, maybe they have a good reason to charge me more.

"Did you let your *boyfriend* win again, Lyn?" a female voice asks through popping static, like an old AM radio station. What? You've never heard of AM radio? Good. That's for decrepit ancient dinosaur losers. Sorry, Dad. I know you liked it, especially for baseball.

I freeze, idly feeling the tingle of my electrical power, always present, just in varying degrees. I mean, *really* varying degrees. "Don't call me Lyn," I say without thinking.

"Don't get testy, *Lightning*," says the crackling voice. Mackenzie Patmina. Who, of course, hates being called "Mackenzie" and goes by just *Zee*. She's somewhere close enough to communicate with me, but for people like us that could be miles.

"I know, he got the big one. But I did pick up two afterward," I say, trying to sound tough. Trying to pretend my accomplishments were more important.

Zee laughs, a popping sound through our strange connection. "And got what? Half the charge he did? Less?"

"Is this the best thing you felt you could do with your time today, Mackenzie? Bother me?"

"I just wonder if you let him win."

Even with our strange connection, I didn't like her tone. "Keep dreaming," I say. "He got lucky. He snuck around me as I hit a bad spot in the field, that's it." I remember almost running into the Stickman and shudder silently.

"Okay, I believe you," she replies, in a tone that makes it clear she doesn't believe me one bit.

———

STICKMEN. Stickmen completely suck. And of course, they're a little terrifying, too. Major zaps of electromagic might have an effect on a Stickman, maybe. If you can hit one. Your average Stickman is faster than it looks.

It? Yeah. Despite the male-centric title "Stick*man*," there is no specific gender to a Stickman. So I call them "It." Mostly because they're creepy. And, deep inside, I hope it pisses them off. Also, because they're creepy.

People like me — electromagicians, or EMs for short — are the only ones who can fend off the Stickmen. We can't necessarily *kill* them, but at least we can try to fend them off long enough to run away, if we're lucky. That's a bit of a blessing/curse problem, since we're also the only ones the Stickmen care about in the first place, the ones they care to attack.

Because the Stickmen are almost magnetized to come for us.

And if they get one of us, they do the most horrible thing possible. They don't kill us, mind you. They do something even worse. They take away the charge, leaving us lost and powerless for the remainder of a sad and empty life. That may sound melodramatic, but look. It's real. There is something profoundly awful about having this power and then losing it. *For you the blind who once could see...* Sorry, I like to do that. Quote and pontificate. Maybe it's my calling. Righto.

Do you have any idea what Stickmen are? They're *me*, just in a *post*-me type of form. Stickmen are people exactly like me, EMs, who should have powers but have been rendered powerless. Well, except for the one caveat that they can still squash an electromagician if they get the chance. Meaning *I* could suddenly be one of *them*.

I do *not* want that to happen. Powerless and strangely genderless, guided by the desire to simply attack EMs and make more Stickmen. Now that's a fate worse than death.

No one knows why Stickmen exist, but then again, no one knows why EMs exist either. We just *are*. There won't be an answer, let it be. By my rough estimate, there are a few thousand EMs in the world. Maybe more, since we're naturally secretive — don't want somebody else gobbling up my charge, right? There are friendly/competitive groups of us, but we don't all get together at a yearly convention or anything. And how many Stickmen are there? Ten? Twenty? A secret underground lair of thousands? Not sure. I've seen one in person. I'd be cool never seeing another.

Besides, I need to get the now-somewhat-banged-up SUV back to the rental place and get the heck out of Dodge. Maybe my brother Kevin hasn't even noticed the charges on his card yet. Rain starts to fall harder, making a sound on the surrounding vegetation like applause. I rev the engine and wheel the vehicle around, but it's making a funny thrum now. Not the throaty, powerful sound it had when I first picked it up. Instead it barks like someone choking on a piece of meat. I rev again and there's a popping noise. Behind me, a spray of smoke and probably corn stalk debris darkens the road, partially obscuring the pair of headlights that appear miles in the distance but gaining quickly.

3

MR. GOLD MUSCLE CAR

I take a left at a random street, simply because I have a hunch. My damaged SUV sputters a bit so I have to press down harder than normal on the gas to get it moving smoothly again after the turn.

I'm suspicious but not really alarmed when the car behind me mimics my turn. Time for Plan B.

What's that? Plan B is simple. Stop the car. So I do it, pulling over to the flat gravel shoulder, my passenger side mirror brushing against the closest stalks of corn. They have a lot of corn here.

The car ambles past me at something close to the speed limit, the driver never once glancing at me as he passes.

That's what gets me alarmed.

The vehicle is one of those American-made muscle car beasts that probably goes 2,000 miles per hour but will suck down a tank of gas faster than a kid with a juice box. And it's gold. Subtle. A gold muscle car. I seriously doubt I can outrun it, especially with my truck wheezing, but I still have the advantage of size. The driver is a light-skinned, burly man with a thick mat of beard covering his chin and cheeks... the kind of beard that threatens to grow right over his eyes, nose, and mouth to finish the job of eating up his face.

All of the roads in the area are long, flat, and straight, and this one's no exception. I watch the gold car fade slowly into the distance. If it was a clear day, I probably could have kept watching him drive straight to the horizon, but on this rainy day, the car is obscured from view after maybe a mile or so.

Time for Plan C.

With my running lights still active, I slowly turn the SUV around and head back the way I came, my eyes glued to the rear view. So far, nothing. Good. If the guy isn't following me, I'll simply cut over to the highway and head to the airport. But I need to be sure first.

I begin to take a left but about three-quarters of the way through the turn, I cut the lights completely, then make it a full u-turn and head straight back to where I was parked just moments before.

If I did it right, the disappearance of my lights in the rainy murk will make it look like I got back on the main road, while instead I sit waiting to see if Mr. Gold Muscle Car will reappear out of the distance.

I don't have to wait long. Racing back toward me, the car comes quickly, lights off. As he goes past me a second time, with our cars now pointed in opposite directions, the driver can't help but gape at me. His cheeks and forehead flush red with anger and embarrassment at the fact that I tricked him. Well, that plus the single finger salute I give him as I stomp on the gas, the SUV spitting up gravel and leaping down the road, putting distance between us.

I figure the best idea — now that I know he's definitely following me — will be to drive fast enough to get lost in the rain, then turn as much as possible. And if that doesn't work, zapparoony, pal. A few warning shots of electromagic should do the trick. You don't mess with an EM. I just don't want to waste it for no reason.

I check the rearview to watch the gold car whip through a u-turn, it's lights blazing back on as it begins to chase after me. At first there's no sound except my own engine, the tires on the wet pavement, and the rain pelting my windshield. But soon, the roar of the muscle car's screaming engine crescendos as its two lights go from pinpoints to twin suns right behind me in no time at all.

Well, I knew I couldn't outrun him.

Plan C.

No wait, I did Plan C already. Plan D? Something like that. Anyway, I stomp on the brakes, and my SUV nose dives toward the pavement, its back end momentarily hopping up and blocking the gold car from view. I hear a screech mixed with a sliding sound and wait for the impact. Going all demo-derby-style, I figure the back end of my SUV can take more abuse than the front end of his racer.

The crash never happens.

Blurring by on my right, bouncing across the shoulder and wiping out a good number of perfectly healthy corn plants, the gold car and its now-even-more-pissed-off driver fly past. I hear thuds and thunks and even catch a few muffled choice words being shouted in my direction.

Then the driver does something pretty slick. He cuts the wheel and brakes, just at the right time, to slam the muscle car not only back onto the road, but also into a sliding stop directly in front of me, spun all the way around in a messy spray of water, mud, and vegetable material.

We sit for a moment, eyes locked, our vehicles nearly nose to nose. Nodding, I give the bearded driver some polite applause, like he just nailed a decent tango on a TV dance show. For a driving stunt, the spin-out/face-off was pretty spectacular, even though I seriously doubt he could do it again in a hundred tries.

I roll down my window a few inches, trying to avoid getting completely soaked, but eager to ask a question. "Hey mister! What the hell do you want with me, anyway?"

As an answer, he presses some unseen button and his driver's side window slides down all the way. A strange grin dawns across his face, and I see that the bearded man has one large, gleaming gold tooth on the right side of his mouth. I'm thinking how funny it is that his tooth matches his car, when suddenly things are not funny at all. He lifts a compact machine gun through the window — the kind you might imagine being used to assassinate some third world dictator — and points it directly at my face.

"Oh, shit!" I shout, ducking down behind the dash of the big SUV just as my windshield is shattered into a billion tiny fragments, like diamonds showering down on my head and back. The gunfire doesn't stop, pummeling into the engine block of the truck with sounds of metal tearing through metal. Hisses and pops seem to come from just inches away. So many bullets. I cower down, eternally thankful for the bulk of the SUV's large front end, and I wait.

Bullets, my friends, are a consumable resource. Eventually, his gun runs out and things all around go silent. Well, except for the sound of the constant downpour and the hissing last breaths of my dying SUV.

At this point, I have to assume that the bearded man is doing a couple of things. First, he's probably reloading. And second, he's probably about to try looking for an angle where the engine block no longer protects my life.

It's time to skip all the other plans and go straight to Plan Z. Zap time.

I ball my fists and close my eyes momentarily, calling the energy up inside me. My body thrums and tingles, and the nearby air is suddenly acrid. Flipping the handle, I kick open the door of the SUV and step out onto the road, with rain now sizzling off my electrified flesh. It sounds vaguely like bugs being zapped in one of those glowing traps at a cookout on a summer night. Bzzt. Bzzt. Zzzzp.

I roll my head around on my neck — it's a sort of habitual tic I do all too often when I'm about to fire off some lightning. Then I step free of the SUV to get a better angle on the gold muscle car, only to find the driver's seat empty. *Where'd you go, Beard?*

Suddenly, the burly man steps out from behind the car. The trunk is up, obscuring him until the last minute, but I don't need to wonder what he was grabbing back there. He holds a sawed-off shotgun, raising it to fire.

Even flowing with electrical power, EMs like me are not bullet-proof. And at a distance of a single car length, that shotgun will riddle me with pellets and I will die. So, at this particular decision point, it's him or me.

I'm vain. I choose me.

Reaching out my right hand and willing my power to flow into it, I snap my wrist to fling an arcing blue bolt of energy directly into the man's chest. A sharp blast rings out as he involuntarily contracts the muscles in his body, including his apparently itchy trigger finger. Thankfully, the various muscles in his arms and upper body also contract, and his shotgun fires harmlessly into the air above my head. I keep shooting electricity into his chest as I hear the shotgun pellets rain down among the corn stalks on the other side of the road, but I know the man is dead. Whether the bolt stops his heart instantly, or sends it into uncontrolled fibrillation, I'm not sure, but the end product's the same.

It's really hard to control the flow of electromagic once it starts, like you're an ant trying to hold onto a blasting firehose. But I don't want to go any further, because it's pointless — the deed is done — and because it's wasting what little power I have left after my failure to get to the F5 tornado first. I struggle to force the energy back down inside myself, tearing my energy bolt away and to the right, willing for it to stop pumping deadly electricity into the man's body.

Finally, the power subsides, and the bearded man thuds heavily to the road face down. Something bounces on the pavement, rolling to a stop near my feet. The gold tooth. "Why?" I ask, though of course he can't answer. "Why'd you have to do that? I don't even *know* you. I didn't want to *kill* you." I shake my head. Sure, I can imagine reasons why regular people attack EMs. I'd heard of it happening before — on rare occasions when a regular stumbles into one of us, it's often so hard for them to rationalize that violence occurs — but I struggle to figure this one out. The dead bearded man in front of me didn't stumble upon me by accident out here in the middle of these corn fields. He targeted me. Why?

Dead men tell no tales, I think as I turn to inspect the two vehicles. EM or not, it was time to flee the scene.

Problem: The SUV is — not surprisingly — shot. I mean, literally *shot*. Like, what appears to be a thousand times. It would never drive again. That leaves the gold muscle car. Just imagine me in a gold muscle car. I silently hope not to run into anyone I know.

Stepping between the two vehicles' front ends, I slide over to the driver's door of the car, then plop myself down to sit behind the wheel. The key is still in the ignition, so I grab it and twist. Nothing happens. I try again, several times. *Shit.* One of the major pain-in-the-ass side effects of firing out bolts of electrical power was that you tend to kill all sorts of nearby electronic equipment. That's how I'd learned to protect my phone in its thick rubber case. When I pulled my lightning bolt from the man's chest, I must have strafed the car by accident.

So, I pensively sit for a while in a stranger's car as the rain falls around me on this remote country road, smelling the bearded man's musty smell and knowing that it would eventually fade to nothing, just as his life had. *Why?*

I slip on my gloves once again and pull out my phone, tapping to call Kevin. It only rings once. "Hey, bro," I say. "You'll never guess where I am." There are some angry words on the other end of the line, and a bit of scolding. Silly me. Kevin is used to following the trail of transactions I put on his credit card, like a kid following breadcrumbs back home through the forest. "Okay, then, maybe you *can* guess." At that point, I just let Kevin yell it out. It's like therapy for him, I think. Besides, I can't easily ask him to arrange my trip home until he's calmed down, anyway, can I?

4

ECONOMY CLASS

Kevin agrees to let me keep my plane ticket home, but nothing more. Which means that I need to figure out a way to hide a dead body and two dead vehicles, then find my way back to the airport. In the rain. In the middle of about 70,000 acres of corn.

I ponder how well and truly my current situation sucks when an idea occurs to me.

Keep it simple, stupid. I start breathing rapidly, in-out, in-out, as fast as I can go. After about a minute of that, when my heart rate is up a good bit, I call 9-1-1.

A man answers the line and asks me what my emergency is, so I take a big gulp of air and just yell. "Oh my God! Please help me!" I add a whimper for good measure. "Some crazy guy tried to run me off the road and then shoot me, and now — and now, I think he had a *heart attack* or something!" I pause, breathing heavily for effect.

"Ma'am, slow down. Please." *Ma'am? Seriously?* I think. *Now I'm a ma'am?* "Where are you? Where did this happen?"

Ah, good question. I pant loudly a few more times. "Uh... I have no idea! I'm lost. There are — I don't know — just corn fields every-where. I was going to check GPS when all the sudden this *car* came out of nowhere — wait! GPS! Can't you find me from this call?" I know he can.

"Generally, yes, ma'am. We can get your approximate location. I'm sending help to your area now — please just stay where you are and try to remain calm."

Remain *calm*? I was going to have to work at it to remain *hysterical*, especially once the cops showed up. Who knows how skeptical they'll be about a would-be random muscle car driving assassin suddenly having a heart attack and dying, but hey, that's my story and I'm sticking to it.

It takes a long time, and the operator urges me to stay on the line the whole time, you know, to ensure I'm okay. But finally, two cop cars, a fire truck, and an ambulance approach, their sirens blaring in the distance long before I see them. I intentionally stand in the rain, dripping wet, to look as helpless and pathetic as possible.

Look on the bright side, I tell myself. *Kevin might not even be charged for the damage to the SUV. Some crazy dude shot it, after all.*

An older officer, probably the one in charge, takes me into his dry vehicle and interviews me, quizzing me a few times on what went down. When he's done, he asks me to stay in the area while they conduct an investigation. I fully plan to ignore that request. But I do give him my real phone number, so technically I'm not completely skipping out.

Things look good when the older officer gives me a blanket and a warm place in the firetruck to sit and recover. Things look even better when he seems to buy my story. "You've been through a lot today. Take all the time you need," he says with a sympathetic nod.

The icing on the cake is when the second officer, a tanned and muscular guy with short dark hair, offers to drive me back to the rental agency. Sure, I don't mind the eye candy, but having him along will validate my story, too. "What did you say your name was again, miss?" he asks.

I smile, trying to look demure. "It's, um, Lyn."

———

ON THE PLANE, I kick back luxuriously into the five inches of personal space I have between the leaning chair in front of me and the angle I'm able to recline my own chair. I think for a moment about the moderately cruel domino effect that happens on planes, where each person slams back their seat, forcing the one behind to follow suit, until the very last hapless soul who can't. Never buy the last seat.

Economy class is a not-so-subtle way of trying to hide my airline purchases from my brother. He can afford first class any time he wants, so I figure that if I buy a cheaper seat, it'll go unnoticed. Unfortunately, it has the opposite effect. Kevin would never buy economy for himself, so any charge from an airline under a thousand bucks stands out like a sore thumb.

And that's fine, Kevin's entitled to first class if he wants it. He's the one managing the family wealth after all. Yeah, I said wealth.

I check my watch — it's of the old-school, self-winding, mechanical variety, by the way; no high-tech digital watches for me, zap zap dead! I see there are still two and a half hours of flight time left. Then 35 minutes in the car, if I'm lucky and traffic is light. Doing the math, I know I can't pop in on anyone tonight, even though I need answers.

Tomorrow, then. Tomorrow morning, I have to get the gang together. Maybe they'll have ideas. Heck, maybe they were attacked, too. Zee and Percival were nearby. Was it a coordinated effort to get all of us?

And if they don't know anything, then I'll go see *the man...* The man everyone knows and loves, at least if you're an EM. People like me practically worship him.

Torden.

In a way, he reminds me of my dad. They might even be around the same age, though with Torden Detonde, it's harder to tell. Unlike my father, Torden has power, and power tends to change the way you age. It could be that Torden is sixty. Or maybe he's a hundred years old. Who can tell?

Oh, and my father's dead. So maybe they aren't all that alike anyway.

Despite the fact that Torden is a kind and generous old man, I don't see him often. I might even be avoiding him. I know. It's me. I don't like charity, and Torden is all about helping other EMs. I just don't want his hand-outs. Something about taking a gift from Torden makes me feel like a failure. Or maybe dirty. Maybe both.

Hopefully Zee has some info. Or Percival. Hopefully, I don't have to go see Torden and suffer through his warm smiles and attempts to *do everything* for me. I can do things for myself.

And yes, I recognize the irony of saying I can do things for myself while sitting in an airplane seat paid for by my brother. But, hey — *I* was the one who stole his card number to buy the ticket, so give me a little credit.

I wriggle on the uncomfortable seat, left, right, left again, finally finding just the right position where I don't feel like my spine might fuse if I fall asleep. As I close my eyes and begin to fade out, the thrifty businessman next to me taps me on the shoulder. Great timing. He needs to pee.

5

AM RADIO

So I mentioned wealth. It's true. My family has had our share, I suppose. I don't have a clue how much money Kevin has, but it's a lot. Enough money that we live in a pretty ritzy townhouse — our parents' home, before they died of course — on the Upper East Side. Enough money that I'm not the least bit surprised to see a driver waiting for me as I exit security at JFK. Wordlessly, he takes my overnight and guides me to the black car waiting outside. Honestly, all this hand-holding makes me itch, but it's at least familiar, so I follow without questioning.

I stare out the window, thinking, as we glide through the night toward Manhattan. The roads all seem familiar, though I can't name any of them. That makes me feel pampered and pisses me off even more. I stare at street signs, thinking this time I'll remember them. But what if I do? Does that really change anything?

Checking my watch, I see it's nearly midnight as we cross the East River. The grey-haired driver — his name is Harry, and I know from experience he rarely talks — never uses GPS, but seems to know instinctually when to detour to navigate New York City's always maddening traffic. Harry takes a right and I realize we're only a few blocks from home.

"Pull over, please, Harry," I say.

I see his raised eyebrows in the rearview. "Ma'am?"

Another ma'am? I sigh. "I want to walk."

Harry isn't *our* driver — we don't have just one. Kevin contracts with a small limo company and they have maybe a dozen or so cars, and at least as many drivers. Still, we usually get Harry or Thomas, the oldest two of the bunch, the ones that had been driving members of my family the longest. Which means Harry isn't surprised by me, either. He knows that I'll sometimes make odd requests, like walking home the last 10 blocks in the middle of the night. He pulls over and gently stops at a corner. "You know the way, ma'am?"

"Of course."

Harry nods. He looks worried, but then he doesn't know I'm an EM. Like most regulars, he doesn't even know what an EM is. "I'll take your bag to the house, then."

I give him a weak smile, embarrassed by his easy and efficient servitude. That's what it is, right? Kevin hires servants, for himself and for me? I feel strangely dirty thinking about it, yet I nod back with a timid thank you and watch Harry depart. He doesn't seem to be an unhappy man. Maybe I should stop feeling bad that he works for us. Or maybe Harry puts on a show because we pay him. Shaking my head, I begin to walk.

After a block, I turn west. Not toward home. Home is north. I'm antsy about what happened and need to talk to someone. As I'm walking, I concentrate within for a moment, pulling up just the tiniest amount of power, enough wattage to send out a signal.

"You there, Zee?" Silence pocked by static is my only reply.

I'm heading west toward Central Park to get a little bit closer, to try to make the connection work, but it's possible my friend simply isn't home. Mackenzie has a studio apartment in the Garment District, west and south of where I am. She complains the place is too small and costs way too much, but she's comparing it to the town-house where I live, which is pretty unfair. I don't pay a cent for it — Kevin manages everything — and we have four posh floors, plus a basement wine cellar and a rooftop terrace. I realize most people think it's to die for, but for me it holds too many memories. Makes me feel small and insignificant rather than cozy and welcome. Meanwhile, Zee can walk from her bed to her refrigerator in 12 steps — she counted. I think she would be much more happy in my house, and honestly, I think I'd be happier in hers.

I get closer to the park, which is probably pointless but somehow I feel it helps to clear a path for my signal. Being near the park always reminds me of the first day. The day in the thunderstorm with mom when I first remember using my power. I must be getting tired, because I'm getting nostalgic.

I open my electric channel to try again. I don't expect an answer, so I allow the old days to guide my words, remembering my dad listening to baseball on the radio. "Now batting for your hometown Electromagicians, *Lightning... ning... ning...* Hop- *kins!*" I add faux cheers. Don't look at me like that. You do weird stuff when you think you're alone, too.

The static pops. "What on earth are you talking about, girl?" Zee sounds sleepy.

I gulp, startled. "Uh oh, did I wake you?"

"Heck yeah. Got back from the airport an hour ago and went right to sleep."

Crap, I think. I need to talk now. "Sorry, Zee, but hey — did anything weird happen to you, when you were out west today?"

She perks up, but only to sound appropriately sarcastic. "Oh yeah, definitely. My friend *gave up* on an F5 so her boyfriend could get a charge. Is that what you mean?"

I shrug off the insult. "No, worse than that." I take a random turn and keep walking. "And I don't have a boyfriend."

"Nothing comes to mind. Why?"

"Um, no reason."

Zee sighs. "Well, Lyn, this has been a lovely chat, but can I go back to sleep now?"

"Sure," I say with a laugh. "Sorry, Zee. We can talk tomorrow. Good night."

"Night," she says and a buzz of static fills the void as she leaves.

Snapping my attention back to the world around me, I realize that I don't know quite where I am. So I stop and turn, scanning for something familiar.

That's when I see the shadowy figure following me.

Quickly, my instincts kick in. *Get out of here, Lightning, or you'll be talking to another cop about another dead body. Even if you did get away with one, you'll never get away with two in a day. Or worse. You'll be the dead one this time.* I was right. I like to think I'm always right. But then I'm biased. I've known me a long time.

Turning around like I hadn't seen a thing, I take a quick right. I'm still hoping to find a landmark, anything I recognize, so I can point myself toward home or at least some place familiar, but for now it seems best just to move.

This is Manhattan, of course. It isn't exactly impossible that someone else was simply walking down the street at night. It's just the *way* the person seemed to be walking — with purpose, directly toward me. My gut tells me something's up. I take another turn, daring a glance over my shoulder.

The dark figure is still back there, rushing to catch up. *Shit, it's happening again. Twice in one day! Why me?*

I hurry to an alley, cutting left and dashing past trashcans. Scurrying rats dart away from me — I must have interrupted their midnight snack. The alley ends in a T and I turn left again, looping back in an attempt to throw off the person chasing me. There's a dark doorway just ahead, so I step into it quietly, trying to vanish.

Waiting in the blackened alcove, I try to calm my breath. No sense hiding if I'm practically blasting trumpet notes with every exhale. I want to fire up my power, but there's a problem. When I'm full of electromagic, it sort of shimmers across the surface of my skin, and that shows up in low light or darkness like a blue glow. If I'm really feeling it, like back in the corn fields, arcs of electricity will zap back and forth wherever two sections of skin are near but not touching.

In other words, EMs can't easily hide in the dark. So I keep my power distinctly and frustratingly turned off.

Time passes, and I wonder if I'm alone. Maybe the guy wasn't following me after all. Or maybe I lost him. Hell, maybe I'll win the lottery using the numbers from the back of the little printed slip in my next Chinese fortune cookie. A lot things are possible. But waiting in the doorway is getting old. I lean out, trying to see if the coast is clear.

"There you are!" a deep voice booms, as a hand reaches out and grabs my arm.

I swallow a scream, stumbling backward and nearly falling. The grip on my arm is strong, keeping me upright. I tense. And without a thought, the electricity rages to the surface. As soon as my power touches the hand holding me, the person jumps back, shocked.

"Ho, now, child, enough of that!" the voice says with a little chuckle. *Laughing? This guy is laughing at me? Who does he think he is? Wait a minute. That voice...*

"Torden? Is that you?" I ask.

The shadowed figure before me steps forward, taking off his hat so that a tangle of grey hair finally appears visible in the glow of an overhead street light. The wrinkled face smiles. "Well, who did you *think* it was?"

6

BE IT EVER SO HUMBLE

"You scared the crap out of me!" I say to Torden, annoyed.

I'm not just ticked off that he made me think he was another stalker — I'm mad at the way it made me look. Like a frightened little baby. I don't like hand-outs and I don't like looking timid. Despite all that, I do sometimes watch sappy, tear-jerker movies, especially if the stars have British accents. Can't help it. Love the accents.

"I'm sorry, my dear. I saw you walking out here so late at night and I just wanted to check that everything was all right with you," he says, the wisps of his scraggly white beard glinting like snowfall in the street lights. "And then, once you ran from me, well, I had to know you were okay." See? Torden's always like that. Always trying to help. It's maddening.

"Well, I'm fine. Thanks for asking, but I think I'm gonna head home now," I say, scanning the surrounding buildings, still unsure of exactly where I am.

"Lyn," Torden begins.

"It's Lightning," I say, not looking at him.

"As you wish," he says, shaking his head with an all-too-fatherly air of concern. "Something's wrong. I can tell. And I know you were out west charge-hunting." Torden seems to know everything all the time, and I never understand how. Oh, and 'charge-hunting' is exactly what it sounds like. EMs hunting for a charge. I glance up at him to see Torden's eyes go wide. "Was it a Stickman? Did you see one when you were out there?"

"What? Huh? No! Not a Stickman. It was a —" Damn it, I'm talking too much. That's making me even more angry at myself.

"It was a... *what*?"

There's no point in covering up. Besides, I already figured I might need to talk this over with Torden. Might as well get it over with it. "A regular. It was a man. Just a regular old person. So I have no idea why he tried to kill me."

"A man? Attacking an EM in broad daylight?" Torden harrumphs, which blows out the whiskers of his grey mustache is an odd wave of facial hair. "He tried to kill you? Are you sure it wasn't just a misunderstanding?"

I smirk. "It wasn't really broad daylight. It was kind of dark and rainy. And maybe he didn't know I'm an EM. Maybe the guy just randomly tries to assassinate strangers with a machine gun."

Torden ignores my sarcasm. "Did he say anything? Give you any reason why?" I shook my head. "Hm. I need to think about this. Strange things are afoot these days. Too many strange things."

"Has something else happened?" I ask.

"What? Oh, yes," Torden says, snapping back to the moment. "An EM in Florida was attacked by two Golems at once."

"Two?" I gasp. *Golem* is the word Torden prefers over *Stickman*, but that seems pretentious to me. And one Stickman was bad enough. Two was, well, it was unheard of. By which I mean that I literally had never heard of such a thing before. "What happened?"

"Her name was Helena Javiera... She was taken. I didn't know her, not personally, but I understand she had a very high Quotient." Quotient is a term EMs use among themselves. It's how much power each one of us can store. Or something like that.

Helena Javiera. I never heard of her before, but I pause, silently, to mourn her loss. Especially if she had a high Quotient. Torden once told me I had a high Quotient, though I always just assumed he was trying to be polite. Could that mean our events are related? The man who attacked me, and Helena Javier being taken? God, the idea makes me shake. Being taken is a fate I fear more than anything — more than death. One moment, you're an EM, the next you're nothing... just... hollow. "Are you saying it was *coordinated*? How's that even possible? Aren't the Stickmen basically mindless machines?"

Torden bobs his head and wags his hands in a noncommittal way, apparently no more clear on the average brain power of a Stickman than I am. "That's what we've always thought, but maybe we're wrong. And if we're wrong..." Torden doesn't need to go further. Intelligent and coordinated Stickmen would present EMs with a clear and direct threat to our existence. "So we have Stickmen seemingly working together, you've been attacked by a regular human, and there's a young EM who hates to get help from anyone who's lost in the city at night." Torden looks down his nose at me with a small, knowing grin.

I didn't know what to say. *Damn, he really does seem to know everything.* Not only is Torden aware that I despise being the focus of his charity, he also knows I'm lost. I feel like a complete and utter fool. "I'm not lost. I mean, not really. The city's a grid. I just need to walk for a bit in some direction and I'll see places I know." Well, it's true. Even if it sounds like an excuse as it comes out of my mouth.

Torden's grin broadens, though it's mostly hidden beneath the hanging mustache. "Well, then perhaps you'll escort this old man in whichever direction you choose so I can find my way home, too?"

"Fine," I say, annoyed, and start to walk us in the direction I think is east. Even worse, Torden makes me promise I'll come talk to him, with my friends, so we can discuss all the things going on. I reluctantly agree before parting ways with him at Lexington and 63rd, assuring him that from there I know my way.

Finally arriving back home, the place looks deserted, dark, and still. The outside light has been left on for me, but I don't see any interior lights as I approach the front door. Reaching out to enter my unlock code, I'm startled as Juliet opens the door with a soft click.

Juliet Charles is our live-in maid. Has been as long as I can remember. She's got 30 years on me, maybe more, but she's remarkably efficient and energetic. More importantly, on nights like tonight, she's nimble, quiet, and, much to my annoyance, ever-vigilant.

Still, I can't help but smile. Juliet lives in her own sort of separated apartment within the townhouse, on the first floor near the kitchen, but her true domain is the front door. Throughout my life, I can't remember getting through it without her knowing. And that's okay. Despite the fact that Kevin pays her — which technically makes her staff and required to be there — I consider Juliet to be my friend. "You waited up for me?" I ask. She simply nods. "Been watching the monitors all night, huh?" I glance at the security cameras that peer down at us from above.

"Ever since Harry dropped off your bag, which was quite some time ago, I must say. And which I unpacked for you, by the way. Did you even bother to change clothes once on your trip? Wait — don't answer that. Besides, you know I can't sleep until everyone's home, safe and sound." *Safe and sound* is a sort of catchphrase that Juliet repeats often. I think she believes that by saying it, it will always be true. She reaches out with one withered but strong hand and ushers me inside. "You must be exhausted. It's so late, and with all your traveling today..." I steal a glance to see if she's chiding me, but she's too good at her job to let something like that show. "To bed, young lady." She apparently has the elevator waiting for me, and practically forces me inside. Yes, we have an elevator. I told you the place was ritzy.

"Good night, Juliet," I say as the doors close and the elevator begins its ascent to the third floor.

———

SOME TIME shortly before noon the next day, I roll out of bed. I'm not a morning person. Why is that even a thing, getting up early? I shiver at the thought.

Sitting on the edge of the bed, I scan the bedroom that I've lived in since my earliest memories. Sheer, mint-colored curtains drape the headboard. A floral pattern wallpaper surrounds me — not your run of the mill department-store kind, but most likely something pretentious from the south of France or Milan or wherever ridiculously ornate, ridiculously expensive wallpaper comes from. To my side is the marble fireplace that I used to love so much in childhood winters, warming the room. Now, I can't remember the last time it was lit. The whole place just shouts *me*, doesn't it? You're right. It doesn't. My room was designed before I was born, and hasn't changed a stitch in my lifetime. With my parents gone, I've mentioned to Kevin that I'd like to redecorate a bit. He won't hear of it. *It would ruin the historic presence of the house*, he always says. What exactly is a historic presence? Sounds like a ghost to me.

It's moderately ironic that my room is the smallest bedroom in the house, and yet makes Zee's over-priced apartment look like a hovel. That's probably why I avoid having friends over. I don't like the way they gawk at all the excess. We have a Victorian-styled dining room for ten. We have a library full of leather couches and probably a thousand books. We have a marble-top bar underneath an etched glass skylight. And of course there's the 300-bottle wine cellar and the rooftop terrace that makes you completely forget you're in the middle of New York City. It's too much. Bad enough I have to see it all the time. No need to subject my friends to this rigid finery.

It stands to reason I'd get the smallest bedroom. Before they died, my parents had the entire top floor. I can't even recall visiting their bedroom when they were alive. Kevin took over the master bedroom once he was lord of the manor (so to speak), but back when we were kids, he had the front bedroom on the third, just down the hall from my room. When he moved upstairs, he encouraged me to take over his old room since it's bigger, but I didn't want it. My place was my place, even though it seemed to be designed for a stranger.

I stand and stretch, then head into the bathroom for a quick shower. I need to get the gang together, but don't want to sound like a chicken shit blowing up their phones with talk of Stickmen armies and gun-toting EM hunters.

Standing in my towel afterward, as drips of water from my legs and hair dot the marble floor, I see my phone start to vibrate, which causes it to shimmy on the granite surface by the sink. It's always set to silent because I hate ringing phones. As it buzzes, the screen lights up with an alert.

Weather Alert: Thunderstorms tonight. Chance of precipitation: 90%.

"That'll do the trick," I say out loud to myself, grinning in the mirror.

7

PERCIVAL'S DRAGON

The sky rolls dark as we drive northwest, heading into Jersey on one of the many expressways I've seen but can't name offhand. This one is marked as I-80. A lot of people give Jersey crap, say it's a mess of industrial horrors tucked within a rat's nest of pavement, and maybe it is in a lot of places. But I gotta tell you, there are definitely some pretty spots, and not too far from Manhattan, either. In forty minutes, we'll be at Garret Mountain, elevation 500 feet or so, which is exactly why we're heading there in a growing thunderstorm.

As the wind picks up, Percival flashes his ridiculously perfect smile at me from the driver's seat, then shoots another grin back to Zee, who's slouched across most of the available real estate behind us. I think Percival takes us to Garret Mountain at times like these because they have a castle there. Pretty sure he likes to play King Arthur or something. That's fine with me — he can have it. I prefer the tower. In places like this, charge-hunting can often be all about elevation. Well, that and luck. Zee actually prefers to walk north to the meadow. She jokes that Percival and I are cheating. And somehow she usually gets a good charge, so she must know what she's doing.

Storms don't always conveniently cross over Garret Mountain —
we have to keep an eye on radar and make some guesses — but
tonight looks very promising. As we travel west, we see dark ominous
clouds — our favorite kind — ahead and to the left, with the charac-
teristic flicker of lightning hopping between them. This is always a
time when everyone in the car is in a good mood, as if we are going to
see a band we all love, or to a dinner spot we all drool over.

Finally, we reach the gate for the park. And of course, it's locked.
Looking at my watch, I see it's 8:52pm — almost two hours since the
park closed. That means the place is deserted, which is perfect. The
park happens to be plopped right in the middle of a normal
suburban neighborhood, so we simply park Percival's car on a side
street nearby and walk in. By the time we step over the low, barely-
there fence, it's really dark out, the wind is kicking, and rain is pelting
us with force. Above, the first tendrils of localized lightning zig and
fork between clouds, lighting up the night like nature's Fourth of
July.

Together, we walk the main park circuit road until we reach the
observation tower lot and part ways. Zee continues north on the road
toward the meadow, while Percival and I make the trek up the short
hill to the tower.

"Sorry about the F5, Lyn," Percival says, looking at his feet while
he walks.

"It's *Lightning*, farmer boy," I say back, though most of my annoyance is feigned.

We're walking close together, and for a moment Percival's hand
brushes across mine. Maybe a tiny bit of his charge seeps through at
that instant, making it feel electric. Or maybe it's something else. I
look at him sideways. He grins again. We pause a moment, then
continue up the hill. If there was something there, we don't talk
about it.

At the base of the tower, we stop. "Enjoy being king of the castle,"
I say.

"Uh, yeah, thanks," he says, strangely nervous. I'm not used to
Percival being nervous.

For that matter, I'm not used to *myself* being nervous, and yet suddenly I realize I am. That brings out my bad habits — natural defenses, I guess you could call them. I look up, seeing the jagged line of a new flash arcing above us. "I need to get up top," I say, turning away toward the tower. "Good luck tonight."

"Hey, Lyn," Percival says, and for some reason I don't even correct his use of my name. "You ever wonder why I like the castle?"

It's a strange question, unexpected. "Um, not really. Because you think you're a king or something?"

Percival shakes his head. "No. It's because dragons are *real.*"

That's it. He just says that and looks at me, like his blue eyes are trying to see through me. "O... kaaaay...," I respond, confused.

He steps closer, pointing up at a fractal of lightning as it cracks and blazes in our vision, momentarily taking away the night. "I mean it. Dragons are real. Dragons are how we get our power." Another bolt breaks the darkness. They're coming fast now, and I'm antsy to get in place. I don't want to miss my chance at a charge. "Think about this storm," he says, swirling one finger around in a circle, pointing at the sky. "This storm is a dragon, get it? It's this giant beast with so much power. No one can slay it. Hell, no one can even slow it down. The storm goes where the storm wants. It's a dragon of darkness and force that bows to no one. And the lightning...," he says, putting his hand on my upper arm and once more making it tingle where we touch. "The lightning is the dragon's tongue, flickering its warning. When the dragon's tongue appears, you can hear it speak in the sound of thunder: *Beware. Great power has come for you. Beware.*" I know what he's saying is ridiculous, but for some reason, laughing is the last thing on my mind.

For a moment, we stand there, only inches apart, Percival's hand unmoving. His eyes are glued to the storm overhead, but he's taller than I am by six inches, so my view is the storm... and his face. Suddenly, the itch I had to go up in the tower isn't so important.

But still, I'm nervous. I shiver.

Percival looks down, into my eyes. "I see someone's excited for the charge, huh?" He smiles again and his hand drops back to his side.

"Good luck, tonight, Lyn." He steps back, then turns and disappears behind the tower, heading toward the castle.

As he goes, I realize I'm holding my hand up in a wave, an awkward smile on my face. I shake my head, turning for the tower and the height I need to get a charge. The storm — Percival's dragon — has come.

———

THE TOWER HAS SECURITY, if you want to call it that. The metal door is locked tight. But for what I'm there to do, I have no need for doors. Reaching inward, I draw upon my power — only enough to get the job done — and I create a glowing blue aura around myself. It's a sort of electromagnetic field, but don't ask me for the physics of how it works. No idea. I just know it does.

I will myself upward and the field lifts me into the air, raising me alongside the rough stone walls of the tower's main turret.

The tower itself has that old-time Medieval look to it, a lot like the castle below. And at the top, there's a round observation deck, my destination. On my way up, I look down the hill toward the castle, trying to see Percival's blue glow as he ascends the same way I am. There's nothing. Maybe he's already at the top. Or maybe he hasn't gotten there yet. I float myself over the edge and gently step onto the top floor of the tower. For a moment, I wonder why Percival doesn't choose the tower instead. It's obviously higher. *Is he letting me have it on purpose? No way. We've been coming here for years...*

The views are amazing from the top of the tower. Though the clouds roil all around me, and flickers of lightning are near constant, I can see the skyline of New York City in the distance, millions of dots of light punctuating the darkness, the greatest, busiest, craziest place in the world. I'm entranced, looking at it. The city I've lived in my entire life. Where I've grown up. The place where I lost my parents.

Distracted, I'm surprised when the first bolt of lightning strikes me. It pulses into the top of my head with a jolt that's momentarily terrifying, then exhilarating. Suddenly, the power is everything to me.

The power, my power, filling me up, washing through me like ecstasy. I hold my hands out, welcoming it.

Then the moment is over.

Lightning is a fleeting thing.

In the aftermath, I breathe deeply, embracing the new power I've gained. There's a blue glow all over my skin as the energy settles in, like water seeping into the ground after a rainfall.

Then it happens again, and again. Three or four times more. Have I been atop the tower for ten minutes? Twenty? With each strike, the glow surrounds me, then slowly fades in. I close my eyes and bask in the new strength I've gained.

The flickering blue at the top of the tower intensifies, and I realize suddenly that I'm not alone. "Hi," Percival says, alighting on the deck beside me. "Nice hunting so far, Lyn." His wavy blond hair is wet from the rain, drooping into his face. He smiles.

I start to speak but no words come out. What's he doing here? Things have always been the same, for years... Zee in the meadow, Percival at the castle, and me in the tower. What's he doing here?

I barely have time to consider it when he steps closer. Percival reaches out and his hands grasp mine. He stands only a couple inches from me. I think he's going to say something, or that I might, but we don't. Then, holding my hands, he looks to the sky.

As if on cue, a jagged bolt of lightning dances between two nearby clouds before it suddenly arcs downward and slams into us both. Holding hands, Percival and I get the charge at the same time, something I've heard rumored but never witnessed. I stand with a look of utter shock on my face, my mouth hanging open.

That is, until Percival leans in and kisses me.

Our first kiss.

Who am I kidding? I'm an aloof loner, a maladjusted rich girl. In some people's opinion, I'm the snottiest person in the world. In other's, I'm the most pathetic. It's my first kiss, period. The kiss and the lightning overwhelm my senses and I fall into a world of nothing but feeling and energy and glow.

In the history of the world, there may be a handful of electric kisses, but I guarantee none compare to this. The lightning sizzles around us and through us, making us as one, pulsing from Percival to me, me to Percival, radiating blue light as we kiss atop the tower with the entirety of the Manhattan skyline before us.

8

THE FUSE BOX

The hours after a big electrical storm are perhaps the most peaceful for EMs, and definitely the best time to find us together. When everyone's charged, everyone's happy. There's less to compete about, less to fight about.

In other words, it's time for an EM party.

We weren't the only ones, by the way, charge-hunting. New York City isn't just one of the largest, most populous cities on the planet for regular humans, it's also home to one of the greatest concentrations of electromagicians on earth. I've heard Tokyo may have more, but I've never been to Japan, so as far as I know that's just hearsay.

Percival drives us back to the city in silence. We don't tell Zee what has happened between us. Sure, we seem mildly giddy, but that's a common emotion among EMs recently recharged. Zee herself is sprawled across the backseat tapping her foot and humming to some song in her head.

I don't need to ask where we're going, because of course we're going to the Box.

The Fuse Box is a sort of bar, but only open once in a while, when the mood strikes. Like now, after the storm. It doesn't have a fixed address, it's just wherever there's space when space is needed. One by one our phones buzz, telling us that tonight's Box is on the 17th floor of a building under massive renovation on the Upper West Side. The whole place is a construction site, sheathed in plastic on the outside, so we could take any floor we want. But there's no fun in putting a bar on the ground floor when the top level has better views. When the Box is open, the Box is loud. That's why it's indoors on the top floor, rather than out on the roof. Best to keep the cops out of our hair.

One other EM bonus: there's no need for electricity. It doesn't matter who brings the lights or the DJ rig, any one of us can provide the power. At times like these, we work out a sort of impromptu time-share plan, where each of us serves as the electrical source for the night, just for a little while, everyone getting a turn.

First, though, we need to get there.

No one in their right mind tries to park in Manhattan, so of course we need to get rid of Percival's car. He drives us back to Engle-wood to park, and we all run into Percival's place for a couple minutes to dry off and change clothes. Percival lives in a basement apartment, the bottom floor of an older townhouse that he rents from a grey-haired couple. They have no idea he's an EM, of course — he just tells them he's a college student, which is kinda true. You know what they say, three-quarters of *life* is *lie*.

As for school, Percival does occasionally take classes at Bergen Community College. But mostly he just earns money doing odd jobs, using his very particular set of skills.

In the same way being an EM won't stop a bullet fired into your chest, it won't pay the bills or get you lunch. Percival does things — things I don't even ask about — to make a living. The only question I ever had for him about it was whether he hurt people for cash. As I have quite recently proven, an EM can be a pretty effective hitman, and in the New York Metro area, you don't have to look very long to find that kind of employment. Thankfully, Percival says he's never physically harmed someone for money. I have to take him at his word and respect his self-imposed limits. Of course, he's never fully clari-fied what he will do for a buck, either, so there's that. He was able to save enough money for the trip out west, so there's that.

After we ditch the car, we have options. The sort of standard commuter way — walk to bus to walk to subway to walk again. That's one. Sounds complicated. Or at least more than I feel like bothering with on this particular night, when I've got a good charge and memories of the top of the tower with Percival are fresh in my mind. "I'll pay for a cab," I say. Though both Zee and Percival raise their eyebrows, no one argues. Why would they? I won't even steal Kevin's credit card this time. I have an expense account of my own. I know, I know. Rich girl expense account. Sorry, it's just the truth. And yeah, I know that having an expense account *and* putting charges on my brother's card don't seem to make sense together. Maybe I'm mostly trying to forget how many things are simply given to me. As they say, *denial ain't just whistling Dixie*. All right, sometimes I make up my own phrases.

The three of us pile into the backseat of the cab with me in the middle, and the driver bounces us through traffic into the city. Half a dozen times or more, a pothole jostles me enough that my skin brushes against Percival and that tingle fires up again. I shoot him a sidelong glance every once in a while, but he just grins and looks out the window.

We ask the cabbie to drop us off a block or so south of the building where the impromptu Fuse Box is happening. No need to advertise that we're breaking into a construction site, right?

Then, approaching the building on foot, Zee checks her phone. "It says the doors on the south side, by the corner, are open. Just push past the construction gate." We do as directed, stepping inside to find Robin waiting.

"Percy! You brought us both dates," Robin says. I laugh. Robin Gordon is an EM from the Bronx. I only see him at the Box, but every time I've met him, he has always cracked me up. He's short, nerdy, and quick with a joke, and he pretends to hit on me and Zee. It's cute. Okay, maybe he's not pretending. Still, he seems like a nice guy, and there's nothing wrong with a little flirting, right?

Percival sees it otherwise, sometimes only barely tolerating Robin's constant attempts at levity. I genuinely think Pers likes Robin, but sometimes their differences stand out. Slapping Robin on one shoulder a little too hard, Percival smiles, their noses only an inch or two apart. "Batman's here now, Robin, my friend. You can tell the *joker* to go home."

"Sure thing, boss," Robin says as Percival steps past him. "But just let me know which girl is Bat-girl..." Robin glances at Zee. "And which one is Robin-girl."

Given the events of the night, the ridiculous question catches even Percival off guard and he laughs. Grinning his perfect grin, Percival turns back and puts an arm over Robin's shoulders. "Come on, pal. Let me buy you a drink. Then we can discuss the women folk." They turn for the door to the stairs. Even with our bodies recharged, it's easier to climb stairs than power an elevator for no reason.

Zee and I just look at each other with raised eyebrows before following.

––––––

THE BOX IS POUNDING AS EXPECTED. Everyone in the room — maybe three dozen of us — is an EM. Mary Tate is mixing drinks in one corner, all oranges and reds and yellows of liquid fun. On the other end of the room, Hayden is spinning tunes wearing sunglasses like this is the biggest rave in history. Bodies bob up and down on a makeshift dance floor as the music throbs against the walls and into our bones like a physical force.

Of all the EMs I know in the city, only a few, like Torden, aren't present. But that's not unusual. Given his age, he's not known to attend our parties.

Hours pass. Despite being a wallflower normally, I actually join the mass of dancing people when Percival nods toward it. The whole time I'm wondering how many eyes are staring at us. How many people know what happened? To one side, I see that Robin has even managed to get Zee to play along — he dances with the kind of energy one might normally associate with someone being electro-cuted. Which of course is not far from the truth here.

The drinks keep flowing and the music keeps playing and the night grows older. Sometimes, despite the general sense of goodwill we all share after a charge, tempers can flare. I don't think that's the EM inside us showing through, I attribute that to our regular human impulses.

Somebody shouts, but I barely notice it. I'm bouncing in time with the beat, Percival next to me. Then things get serious.

A bright blue blaze lights the room from one end, by the door to the stairs. Then there's another, just to the side.

Oh dammit, a fight? I think. I'm not the only one to think it.

"Hey, break it up!" someone shouts lazily. EM fights are pretty pointless — one EM shooting his hard-won electromagic into the other, like a gift.

"No fighting at the Box!"

"Cut it out, you two!"

There's a commotion and lots of bodies angling, trying to see. I'm near the back, so nothing is clear to me. Just the blue lights, hovering near each other, lighting up the far walls. Percival and I stop and stare.

More shouts.

Finally, DJ Hayden looks up, his headphones drooping to his neck. He reaches out and turns a knob, silencing the music between beats.

In the sudden quiet, I can hear words from the far end of the room finally.

"Get back! Get back!"

What the hell is going on?

There's a thumping noise, from the door to the stairwell. Another blue blaze fires up near the door, then one more.

"It's here! Back up!"

It? I think, fuzzy from the charge and the dancing and the drinking and the night of events started by Percival's kiss.

With a loud, echoing thud, the door slams open. Something zips into the room like a shadow blown by a hurricane, and bolts of electricity fly from several sources, crossing like heat lightning on steroids. The dark shadow curls around the arcing energy, evading them all, before momentarily coming to rest in one corner.

There, the thing stares out at us, scanning back and forth. With an urgency that stops my heart, it locks its grey, dead eyes on me. I can't believe what I'm seeing.

A Stickman has come, and I'm trapped.

No, not just me. Now there are several dozen EMs suddenly trapped on the 17th floor of an empty building.

I swear the thing smiles before leaping into the crowd.

9

SPONGE

Dark and light, shadows and electricity, alternating, bouncing off the walls. Light streaks out toward the dark, trying to obliterate it. Dark swoops back in and the light retreats.

Poetic, huh?

Well, not so much when your life's at stake. Everyone in the makeshift nightclub — including me — freaks out.

Pockets of space alternate between blinding brightness and blinding darkness as the room turns into an insane churn of bodies diving, powers flaring, a dark thing reaching for us one by one, and all of us doing anything we can to evade that touch. Shouts and screams of every timbre echo through the cavernous room.

The Stickman desperately seeks a victim, and we all desperately try to get away. Never has the Box seemed a more appropriate name. We're all stuck inside.

Glass shatters behind me. EMs are breaking through windows to escape, zipping themselves out into the night air, each surrounded by a blue glow that recedes quickly as they race away. I know they can't travel that way for long — not in downtown Manhattan. Way too easy to be seen. Anyone looking up at the building right now has got to be wondering what sort of crazy electrical problem or light show is going on. Someone's probably already called the cops. Or maybe not. It is New York, after all.

Instinctively, I fire a bolt of power at the Stickman. It dodges and then lunges in my direction. Well, now. Seems that attacking a Stickman draws it to you. Who knew? Just a little something to remember, you know, if I live for more than another few minutes.

Percival grabs my arm, and even in the frenzy, I feel the tingle where our skin touches. He points, and I see other EMs racing out the door. I nod.

Using my power to make a direct connection, I call out to Zee. "Where are you? Can you head for the stairs?"

"Way ahead of you," Zee replies, and I see a dark form with her bobbing hairstyle in silhouette running for the exit. Next to her is another EM, short, wiry and male — Robin.

More bolts crisscross the room and EMs scatter in every direction. The Stickman circles, finally bringing its attention to Hayden. For some reason, Hayden is still behind the DJ table, which is suddenly the only thing between him and eternal zombification at the hands of the Stickman. The thing sizes him up and steps closer, almost reveling in the chance to slowly take Hayden's power.

I start to go back — I can't leave Hayden to the Stickman even though we barely know each other. Doesn't matter. New York EM solidarity, I guess. 2-1-2. Besides, how little I know someone is likely a reflection on my hermit-like lifestyle, not the other person. So I'm about to turn back when Percival tugs on my shoulder. "Wait. Look." He nods in the direction of the table and I see that Hayden's hands are resting on the controls, just like he's about to...

The Stickman is within feet of Hayden, and seems to be smiling, though its face remains dead and its eyes are empty and black. It pulls itself inward, preparing to spring.

And Hayden suddenly pushes all the controls forward.

A blast of noise erupts, turning instantly into painful, ear-splitting feedback. The Stickman falls back, curling inward to avoid the assault of sound. Hayden takes his chance to flee, racing toward the door.

"Go!" Percival shouts, giving me a solid shove forward, and I run, covering the length of the huge room in seconds, not daring to look back.

In front of me, Zee and Robin are already in the stairwell, but they're turned around, gesturing wildly for us to hurry. "Come on! Let's go!"

From one side, Hayden reaches the door first and dashes between Zee and Robin, not pausing. He hits the stairs and just keeps going, disappearing from view.

Moments behind him, I pass through the doorway with Percival breathing down my neck. We push into the small space beside Zee and Robin and pause to catch our breath. Back in the room, the Stickman is nowhere to be found. In fact, the room seems to be completely empty, the last of the EMs probably shooting out the window after Hayden's aural onslaught. Percival slams the door shut behind us.

Robin looks over the edge of the staircase. "Hayden! How did you know that would work?" he yells downward with a cheeky grin.

"I didn't!" Hayden's voice calls, out of breath, from somewhere far below.

Robin turns to us. "Well, we should get the hell out of here, too. Ladies?" Always the joker, he gestures dramatically for Zee and I to go first, which we do, heading down the stairs quickly. "I mean *all* the ladies...," Robin says, smiling toward Percival and batting his lashes ridiculously. Percival just rolls his eyes and follows after us.

At the first landing, we turn and see Robin still holding his silly pose at the top of the stairs.

There isn't time to shout. No time for him to run. The door blasts open and the Stickman falls on top of Robin and it's over. Robin shrieks and drops to the floor, trying to fight off the creature with electromagic. It's no good. The thing touches him, and its touch saps his power. The Stickman turns toward us, both a warning and a gloating sign of victory, as its body tenses, pulling all the juice out of Robin like a hideous sponge.

Robin's body jumps awkwardly and tendrils of smoke curl upward as he is charred, burned alive from the expelled electricity. He screams in pain, but the sound weakens and cracks as his skin darkens and his eyes burn out to black orbs. The smell is beyond revolting.

Percival turns back toward us. "Go! Go now! There's nothing we can do now but *move!*"

For a moment, Zee and I are too stunned to take a step.

"If you two don't run, pretty soon we face *both* of them at once!" Percival says. *Both?* I think. *Oh yeah. The Stickman* and *Robin.* Somewhere in the back of my mind, I wonder if that explains the two Stickmen who attacked the EM in Florida. The thought of it shakes me into action.

Without another word, Zee launches herself down the stairs two at a time, sometimes even more, jumping to the next landing and turning as fast as she can to hit the stairs once more. I do my best to keep up, with Percival always right behind me.

As she takes a turn near the bottom of the stairwell, I realize Zee is crying. Not simple tears, but big, bawling sobs. I knew she liked Robin — we all did. But maybe I underestimated how much he meant to her. I look away, not wanting to embarrass her.

In the repetition of run, jump, turn, repeat, I find myself burning inside, my mind wandering while my body does all the work.

Someone tried to kill me — some regular human. Plus, Torden told me there had been coordinated attacks by Stickmen. And now, we were attacked and my friend is gone.

Pounding down to the last landing, we slam through the door and out into the night air. Sirens approach from somewhere in the distance. What do you know? Someone actually called the cops.

Once out of the building, we turn and walk into an alley, being sure to take a few random turns as we put distance between ourselves and the building. As if she's finally able to react, Zee turns her head upward and howls at the sky, a sound of anger and anguish and frustration. "Damn it!"

"Zee —," Percival begins, but she cuts him off.

"No, don't try to rationalize it, Percival, or make everything okay. Robin is gone for no good reason. Those stupid *mindless* things." Zee spits her words out in anger.

My fists clench tightly and little arcs of electricity zap between my knuckles. "Someone's going to pay for this shit. That's a guarantee," I growl.

Zee turns. "How? How exactly? Stickmen just wander around, until they get our scent, and then try to take us. There's no *meaning* to it. There's no point. There's no way to stop them because there's no one to stop." She throws her hands downward in disgust. "Nothing we can do about it matters one bit. Robin is gone for *nothing*."

What can I say in response? I've always known the same reality, ever since I became an EM. Stickmen are what they are, and nothing more. But things — weird things — have been happening. Is it really just a coincidence?

"I don't know, Zee. I mean, that's what we've always been told. But maybe there's something more going on," I say to her, trying to appear calm, so my anger doesn't seem like it's directed at her.

"What are you talking about?" Percival asks. Finally, I tell them both about the man who tried to kill me out west, and Torden's story of the EM in Florida attacked by multiple Stickmen.

"Why didn't you tell us all this before?" Zee asks.

I shrug. "I was going to... but there wasn't time, and it all seemed kind of random, anyway." Actually, I'd planned to tell them when we left Garret Mountain. Percival's unexpected appearance on the tower must have derailed my mind.

"Okay, so what if there *is* something or someone behind this," Percival says. "How do we even begin to find out who?"

"No idea," I said, shaking my head.

Zee stops, pulling out her phone. "Well, I know one thing. We've got to talk to Torden. He may know more than he told you." She starts to make a call.

Five minutes later, I'm hailing a cab to take us across town.

10

IN THE COURT OF THE KING

We get dropped off in Co-op City, which is about as close as we can get without arousing suspicion. Then we walk down to the Hutchinson River and quickly zip ourselves across with a little EM power. Three glowing blue bursts skim the water — and no, it's highly doubtful that anyone is watching. If you've ever been to Co-op City, you know that night fishing is not big there. Or day fishing, for that matter. Once on the other side, we're back to walking, and it's notably darker than downtown. We head through a park, past a golf course, with the trees doing wonders to block out the city lights and the night sky. After a while, we come to a split and head left, soon finding Torden's place looming above us, casting pale shadows amid the shades of blue and grey that make up the nighttime world. It's so quiet here, especially at night.

"I always forget how far away this Transylvanian castle is," I say to no one in particular, mostly just to break the silence. Percival and Zee give me funny looks, so I shrug and shut my mouth for the rest of the walk. That doesn't help much. It just gives me more time to think about how weird this all is.

Let me explain. Torden has a rather unusual home. If you can even call it a home. For a few decades, from what I heard, he was night security manager at a place called Orchard Beach. What the heck is Orchard Beach? I'm not surprised you'd ask. Most people have heard of Coney Island, or maybe Brighton Beach. Orchard Beach is nowhere near those. First off, it's in the Bronx. Second, it's man-made. And third, it had its hey-day about 80 years ago.

Looming over the sand and water is a monolithic curved building called the pavilion, split in half to allow beach-goers to stroll down the center. Ten years back or so, the pavilion at Orchard Beach was boarded up and chain-link fence was installed all around to keep people out. It might have been due to the fact that the place looked like an errant sneeze could knock it down. And I've got to tell you, ten years of neglect have not improved its structural integrity. In my few previous visits to the pavilion, I had the pleasure of dodging falling bits of concrete on at least three occasions.

Disregarding all that, and realizing it's a place of almost complete privacy, at least indoors, Torden took up residence in the northern half of the pavilion. No one seemed to remember that he had keys to everything, once it was condemned. Getting in wasn't even hard. And because he had worked there so long, he got shifted to another job in the park, so no one's even surprised to see him come and go all the time, though I'd have to guess his employment was long over by now.

During the warm months, there's a never-ending stream of humanity flowing toward the beach, so there's no problem for EMs to slide into the crowd, then disappear into the welcoming confines of Torden's pavilion. And during the colder months the place is practically deserted. It's a perfect ruse.

Torden turned the building into a sort of commune. From the outside, it still looks like a crumbling architectural nightmare of massive, stark columns. But inside...

Well, okay, inside it's probably worse. But it's *spacious*. An almost ridiculous amount of room for Torden to stretch the muscles of his generosity. He has dozens of rooms prepared, for permanent EM residents as well as transients. You don't even have to offer a reason why you need a place to stay. Any EM who walks through the door gets a room, no questions.

We skirt the parking lot by a wide margin, avoiding the handful of cars filled with couples seeking privacy in a crowded city. As we round the north building, a female voice speaks to us, crackled with bits of static. "If you've come in peace, raise your left hand." It's the standard test. Regular humans can't hear our electromagic communications. Zee, Percival and I stop and raise our hands. Consider it the secret hand shake or our gang sign. Never mind that we just look like three over-eager kids trying to answer the teacher's question in class. "Just you three?" the voice asks over our weird connection.

"Yeah," Percival replies out loud. Nearby, there's a metallic click and then a dull thud. A rusty door — something you'd think would groan with any movement — swings outward almost silently. Creaking doors at an abandoned building in the middle of the night would be a dead giveaway.

Two EMs I've never seen before pop out and stand to each side of the door. Add the female watcher above and that means there are at least four EMs who weren't at the Fuse Box, if you include Torden. Lucky them.

From the dark interior, Hayden appears, frazzled but fine. It's not surprising he would run back here after the mess at the Box. He's one of the EMs that make the pavilion his regular home. "Hey guys — glad you made it out. That was unreal, and — wait. Where's Robin?"

Zee looks at her feet, and Percival shakes his head slowly.

"No! No way, not Robin!" Hayden holds his head in both hands. "I can't believe it. Him? A Stickman now?"

"We need to see Torden," Percival says.

"Yeah, of course, come in." Hayden gestures for us to follow as he leads us into the dark hallway. He heads toward the far end as the main door is closed behind us and we're plunged into complete darkness.

The slightest blue glow appears ahead. Hayden uses just enough power to light the way, reaching out for the next door and twisting the handle. Then, he douses his light as a world of flickering orange floods in.

Inside Torden's pavilion, they've tried to put a shine on the proverbial turd, but the turd still shows through. The walls are cracked and crumbling in places, which is either barely hidden or possibly accentuated by the massive amount of candles on display. I know from experience that Torden reserves the use of electromagic for only the necessities. Even Hayden's brief use in the hallway would probably make Torden wrinkle up his already-wrinkled forehead.

Hayden leads us past rows of candles and a few EMs from the party who have also raced home after the fiasco. As we pass them, a few ask if everyone got out okay and each time, Percival gets to be the bearer of bad news. Soon, we're trailing a flock of people as we climb the stairs to Torden's antechamber.

That sounds fancy, doesn't it? If you pictured a wide room ornately decorated with royal tapestries and such, you'd only be slightly off. There's no throne, but Torden often sits in a large, antique chair on one end of the room. Antiques are kind of his thing, and the more carved and complicated the woodwork, the better. Other benches, chairs and tables sit to each side, but the center is reserved for a wide row lined with candles on tall pillars, leading directly to Torden's chair.

Hayden guides us forward, then slips into the growing crowd, leaving us before the man himself. It all seems excessively formal to me. Can you tell why I hate coming to this place? There's something about the in-your-face nature of Torden's generosity combined with his pomp and circumstance that rubs me the wrong way.

An older EM named Rand stands to one side of Torden's chair. *The king's advisor*, I've taken to calling him. Rand seems humorless and calculating, to me, but I barely know him.

"Percival," Torden says in his deep voice. "Mackenzie. And Lyn." He nods to each of us in turn, but it feels like he's lingering on me, which makes me uncomfortable. "I have been told of the great tragedy and loss of this evening. That our friend Robin has been taken. We need to hold a remembrance."

A murmur of agreement goes up from the assembled crowd, and soon we leave the dark interior and flow toward the colonnade that curves along the outside of the building, facing the water. The beach is deserted at this time of night, except for a few couples arrayed at distances from each other, far to the sides. The beach is over a mile long, so even if they see what's about to happen, it's unlikely any of it will make sense to them.

We silently stand in the cool air of night and Torden faces the water. He raises one hand toward the sky and a tiny white dot of electromagic floats up from his palm, like a spark flittering away from a campfire at night. Beside him, Rand repeats the gesture, and then we all join in.

Our flecks of electricity fly into the air in a rough cloud, mostly in shades of blue, though some are closer to white like Torden's. My own appears white as well, with only a tinge of blue. As I let it go, I think of Robin and his horrible fate, the horror that he has become. *Does Robin even remember us? Does he remember his life anymore?*

Some of the dots fade out quickly, mostly from the EMs that have most recently discovered their power. Others linger, like mine, Rand's, and Torden's, floating ever higher into the sky. Remembering Robin, a tear forms in the corner of my eye, and I tilt my head down to wipe it away. That's when I notice Torden. He seems to be following my spark, almost analyzing it.

As I wipe at my eyes, the last of our lights wink out. Through tear-blurred vision, I don't notice whose spark disappears first.

Torden approaches. "Lyn, I think it's time we talked about some things. Don't you?"

I have no idea what *things* Torden wants to discuss, but I have a lot of questions. What is it that he knows? Are recent events just coincidence, or part of something larger? I follow him back inside, with my friends trailing behind.

11

THE ANGER QUOTIENT

"Lyn, my dear girl, you are special," Torden says, smiling warmly. Still, I don't exactly feel charmed. His hospitality has always rubbed me the wrong way. My hang-up? Sure, fine, whatever. My hang-ups and paranoia have gotten me this far. I'm gonna stick with them.

He sits in his broad, antique chair, with his advisor Rand to one side, candles throughout the large room creating a moving mass of light and dark. Meanwhile, Zee, Percival, and I stand. Is humble pretentiousness a thing? Because I think Torden has it mastered. "My name is *Lightning*," I say, annoyed. Does Torden grin even wider as I say this? I almost think he does. But I brush that aside. "And I assume you're talking about my Quotient again, right?"

"My apologies, *Lightning*," he says. "How do I keep forgetting? And yes, I mean your Quotient. Do you know what it really means, this word 'Quotient'?"

I shrug. "Yeah, I think. It's how much power an EM can hold, right?" I look at my friends, but neither offers any input. I guess we're all on the same page, which is to say relatively clueless.

"Not exactly," Torden says. "An electromagician's well of power is somewhat related to body mass, though even I am not sure precisely why. A small child will inherently have less ability to store electricity than an adult, but it's not strictly about mass. I have seen very, very large men — men you'd almost call giants — with less ability to hold on to power than a rail-thin waif. For the most part, though, the word Quotient doesn't apply to the *amount* of power an EM has, but instead their *efficiency* with that power."

Well, that certainly clears everything up, right? I glance at Percival and see he's lost, too. "And that means...?" he asks.

"What it means, Percival, is that if you and Lyn — sorry, Lightning — were to absorb the exact same amount of energy, *she* could use it longer and with greater efficiency." Torden grins at Percival to drive home his point.

Percival huffs a bit, like he doesn't believe it. Do I believe it? Thinking back, I remember some of our trips to Garrett Mountain — times when we all should have received about the same charge — and afterward, Zee and Percival seemed to run out before me. Why? I always assumed it was because they used their power more than me, but now I wonder.

"But, does that mean she's stronger?" Zee asks.

Torden shrugs. "That depends on what you mean by stronger, Mackenzie. If everything else was equal? Yes, our Ms. Hopkins would outlast and outperform you and Percival with her electromagic. But don't feel bad. She'd beat everyone here in such a competition." By this time, people start turning heads. People start noticing what he's saying. "With the possible exception of me, of course." Torden sits stone-faced, his smile suddenly gone. "And maybe Rand." Beside Torden, his sidekick shows no reaction.

Murmurs go through the crowd and suddenly I feel like every eye is on me. That everyone is analyzing me. It isn't a nice feeling. I'm used to being an outcast and a loner, but on my terms. Now, I feel like Torden is putting me on the spot. His words are making the others look it me in a new way — like I'm not one of them, not anymore. More like I'm someone they shouldn't trust. I should have known not to come to this place, not to talk to Torden. He may have answers, but I'm learning the hard way that I might not like the answers he gives.

I shake my head. "What are you talking about? I'm no different than anyone else." I scan the EMs around the room, ending with Percival and Zee, but I don't see a lot of nodding. "Anyway, what difference does it make? This isn't exactly a competition."

Torden smirks. "You're right. We are not in competition with one another, but..."

I interrupt him. "And it isn't like I'm so great that I saved Robin back there at the Fuse Box, when that Stickman attacked us."

"Like I said," Torden begins, "you would likely outlast and outperform others here. But that doesn't mean you can do anything you want. If a Golem were to touch you... Forgive me. I know you all prefer the name *Stickman*. But to me, that seems like somewhat of a slur."

"So now we need to use manners with those things?" Percival jokes. Around the room, a few people laugh.

Torden doesn't look amused. In fact, he looks angry. But he continues. "Lyn, if a Stickman were to touch you, I suspect you'd fare no better than any of us. Having a large Quotient doesn't mean you can dodge bullets or come back from the dead."

"Then what the hell is it good for, anyway?" I ask, roughly.

Torden pauses, idly smoothing one sleeve and straightening his shoulders. "How old do you think I am, Lyn?"

I blink. *How old? Fifty? A hundred?* Torden had been around since the beginning for me. I couldn't say for sure, but he always seemed the same, almost ageless. "I... have no idea."

"I'm two hundred and six this year," Torden announces, for all to hear, and the crowd gasps.

Looking across the sea of faces, I realize only two are wrinkled. Only Torden and Rand. No, wait. There's another, almost hiding in the back — a friendly guy I've chatted with once or twice but otherwise barely know, Walter. Still, wrinkled faces are by far the minority in the room. I never noticed how young the rest of us were until now. "How is that possible?" I ask.

"Quotient, of course," Torden replies. "I am more efficient with my electricity. And it has made me live longer. A lot longer."

I'm shocked. I knew electromagic messed with the way human bodies age, but I'd never heard of something like this before. I thought Torden was closer to my dad's age, in his sixties or maybe a little older. But not two hundred. No way. It's almost impossible to comprehend what he's saying, to imagine the things he's seen in two hundred years. "And Rand?"

"Oh, I don't recall precisely," Torden says with a smile. "Do you, Rand?"

Beside him, his second-in-command is as stoic as always. Rand speaks, but in a short bark, almost like it goes against his nature to make a sound. "One hundred fifty eight."

Torden chuckles softly. "It seems I was an old man before you were even born, my friend." Rand remains expressionless. Rand is kinda like that.

My mind whirls. They're *so old*. And Torden is telling me that I'm like them. I never considered what it might feel like to be told I'm immortal. Now I was trying to keep from passing out at the news. I'm practically gasping for air, like a drowning woman. I know it's crazy, but I'm thinking of Percival's kiss. If we were together, how long would it last? How long would *he* last, if I lived on and on? "Is this what I can expect? To live forever? To be immortal?"

Torden bursts with laughter. "*Immortal*? Who said any of us were immortal?" he asks.

"Isn't that what you're telling me?" I say, between gulping breaths.

Leaning forward, Torden looks deeply into my eyes. "Lyn, all I'm saying is that, if you use your Quotient, your efficiency, you can last a long time. But if you think death no longer waits for you, as it does for us all, I'm afraid you're mistaken."

I think for a moment, but what's the difference, really? I didn't walk into the room thinking I was immortal. It wasn't exactly going to ruin my day to find out I was already right, that I could most definitely die. "Okay, fine. I'm mortal like anyone else. Good. I can't imagine how bored I'll be in a few hundred years," I say before realizing my words might be taken the wrong way. "No offense."

Torden smiles. Rand doesn't. "None taken, my dear. But if you ever reach my age, you might be surprised how much there is to do. And how much you like doing it."

I shrug. No sense even trying to wrap my head around such things. I have something more important to say. "Tell me this, then. You've been around for 200 years. How do you... *fix*... one of them?"

"One of *what*?" Torden asks.

"The Stickmen. How do you do it?"

"Fix it? What do you mean? Return Robin to himself? I'm afraid that's simply impossible," Torden says with a strange gleam in his eye. I know from past experience that Torden loves theoretical discussions. Perhaps annoyingly too much.

His words make me shudder. "Fine. If it's too late for that — too late for Robin — then I just want to know how I can help him find peace. How can I help Robin?" In the crowd around us, there are mixed reactions. Gasps. Disbelief. And, more importantly, some nods. Several EMs repeat my words. *Help Robin.*

Torden wrinkles his forehead, studying me. "Robin is gone, dear. Why risk your life? If you get too close to him, or any other one of the Golems, you yourself could end up like him." Something about his tone strikes me as odd.

"Just tell me how. How to put Robin out of his misery. For his sake." I cross my arms, though with Torden I doubt my gesture feels intimidating. It seems pretty clear he doesn't want to tell me, and it's certain that my pose isn't going to give him a change of heart. But he does. The eager faces of the others around us, their murmured sentiments — that's what sways him. Is Torden susceptible to peer pressure, or is this just some political game for him?

"Fine, but I don't recommend it. I recommend you steer well clear of any Golem — Stickman — you encounter. But *if you must*... If you must try, then you must put all of your effort into it. All of your electromagic. Because Stickmen are like many other things that conduct electricity — or that store it."

I shake my head, not following. "*Put all my effort into it*? That's it? Why? What does that do?"

Torden raises both fists and presses his knuckles together at eye level. "Overwhelm the circuit and —" Abruptly, he explodes his hands outward. "It breaks down."

I shake my head, but at least I have an answer. If I ever find a Stickman — if I can find Robin — I will put every ounce of my power into ending it. I feel like it's the only way to save Robin's soul, if that truly is a thing.

Torden once again chuckles softly, his hands waving loose circles in the air. "Of course, there's still one problem."

"What's that?"

He looks into my eyes with a deep seriousness. "It's only *theory*, my dear. In all my lifetime, I can assure you, I have *never* seen another electromagician actually do it and live."

12

NIGHT BOATS

We leave Torden's strange, candlelit lair behind. "As much as I'd like to be alone, I realize it's probably a bad idea," Zee says in a low voice as we exit the pavilion. After his guards escort us out, they slip back inside and close the eerily silent door behind them, leaving us alone in the dark. "But I have to do something. Especially since we're here."

"What does that mean?" Percival asks, your typical clueless male. I shoot him a look that tells him to keep his mouth shut, then nod to Zee, encouraging her to do whatever she needs to do. Zee leads us into the darkness, and then in a long curve around the north end of the pavilion, well out of sight of anyone who might be there after dark.

She takes us to the beach, walking south, out into the wide sand. After a few minutes, my eyes adjust, but still it's hard to distinguish between what might be a shadow in the sand or a washed up log, rather than a couple looking for privacy. Thankfully, we find shadows and debris, but no people. Zee continues down the beach in the darkness, turning like she's trying to find something. Percival almost says something again, but I give him a quick jab to the ribs to remind him to stay quiet. Finally, Zee locates a lone rocky mass that sticks up out of the sand, and aims for it. When we get to it, she turns and sits down, staring out into the water.

Percival, probably wisely, decides to wander off for a bit and give us a moment. I sit next to Zee, but remain silent, waiting for when she's ready.

"We came here, one time," she says eventually.

"Yeah?"

Zee turns to me smiling broadly, but the moonlight reflects off the wetness on her cheeks. Out in the water, two boats quietly cross paths in front of us, far enough away that their engine noise is drowned out by the lapping waves. A red light glints from the boat heading north, while the southbound vessel shows green. They pass like a weirdo slow motion Christmas light display.

"We were both at Torden's pavilion one night, and Robin asked me if I wanted to sit on the beach with him. Of course, he did it in that over the top, flirtatious way he always spoke to me, but..."

"But what?"

"I liked it." Zee looks down and I put a hand on her back gently. "I liked *him*."

I don't say anything, I just slowly rub Zee's back, a gesture that says I care, knowing any words I say won't change how she's feeling. Sometimes you just gotta let someone talk.

"You know what's sad?" she asks after a moment.

"It all is, the whole thing," I say.

"No, of course it is, but the saddest thing is this. I always assumed there was time. Time to do my thing, for him to do his, and time for us to figure it out, eventually. Maybe there was going to be something between us, but now there never will be. We're nothing more than those two boats out there, just passing our separate ways."

Out in the water, the night boats slowly separate, getting farther and farther away from each other. The symbolism isn't lost on me, or on Zee. I can feel her body shaking as she cries.

Suddenly, Zee bursts out with a sharp laugh that sounds like pain. "God, would you listen to me? I sound like some pathetic, sappy love song. *Ships passing in the night.* What the hell is wrong with me?"

I eye her sideways with a grin. "It isn't wrong to care about someone, Zee, even if what you said totally sounded ridiculous. Embarrassing even. You should apologize to Robin."

Zee lets loose another painful burst of laughter, raising her hands toward the night sky. "I'm sorry, Robin!" And then we two girlfriends lean into each other, embracing while we laugh and cry at the same time. "I'm really sorry, Robin," Zee says into my shoulder.

"So am I," I say.

———

"YOU GUYS SEE THAT? I thought the south wing was closed," Percival says from somewhere behind us, once again oblivious to the moment he's stepping on.

Zee pulls back from our hug, wiping at her cheeks, but smiling still. She typically wears more makeup than I do, and now her mascara is a blurry mess, blending into the shiny wetness on her face. She dabs at her bottom lids but still has the composure to roll her eyes at Percival's apparent dense behavior. "What is it, Pers?"

Coming up to us quickly, he waves both hands, palms down. "Shh! Quiet down! Something's going on over there," he says, pointing back toward south wing of the pavilion. Extending from the building itself is a low brick-walled structure that blocks off the south yard. It's some sort of equipment storage area. In the middle of that brick wall, there are gaps surrounding the Orchard Beach Snack Bar, which is, of course, closed and shuttered. But to the right side of it, the side closest to the pavilion's south wing, a faint but distinct glow is visible. Someone must be in the yard, though at this time of night that seems unusual. "And don't call me *Pers* — I told you, it makes me sound like a handbag."

"It's just a light, what's the big deal?" I say, yawning. I'm ready for the night to end. My room at home, despite its woefully out-of-time decor, is calling to me. Given the late hour, I hope that Juliet hasn't been waiting up for me. Again. But I know she will be.

"I want to check it out," Percival says, starting to walk toward the glow. Zee and I share a look then shrug. We stand up, dusting the sand off our clothes, then follow after him.

Percival is taking the whole moment way too seriously, creeping along like a spy in some war film, infiltrating behind enemy lines. If he could take other things in life anywhere near this seriously, maybe he wouldn't be so maddeningly *male*. He's half crouched as he nears the snack bar, using trees and benches along the path to block our approach. Personally, I think the likelihood of someone standing guard over a food stand with no food is pretty slim.

Sure enough, we reach the snack bar without raising any alarms. The glow is now clearly a light coming from somewhere inside the south yard, closest to the south wing of the pavilion building itself. Percival stops at the edge of the wide opening that leads into the yard like a S.W.A.T. team member about to burst into some crime lord's headquarters.

Stopping behind him, with Zee trailing me, I tap Percival on the shoulder. He turns and gives me a too-serious look, raising a single finger to his lips. I return the look with a furrowed brow, then point at him silently. I begin making gestures with both hands, diagramming some outlandish plan for the three of us to split up and break in, ending with my most dramatic move — two fingers pointing at my eyes, then twisting my hand around to point at Percival. *I'm watching you*. Of course it's all faux spy mockery, but it takes him at least thirty seconds to realize I'm yanking his chain. He sighs, and behind me, Zee stifles a laugh.

"What are we doing this for?" Zee says, until Percival dramatically and silently urges her to stop talking.

He leans toward us and talks in the lowest of whispers. "I'm going in. You two stay here if you want."

Zee isn't having it. "Pers, if you walk in there and it's some grounds crew member prepping to comb the beach or whatever, you're gonna scare the shit out of him, and then he's gonna call the cops on us. Let's just go home." I nod my agreement.

"Ten seconds, no more," he says. "I'll be careful, and I'll be right back." Without waiting for a reply, he turns and ducks into the opening.

I look at Zee with that all-too-familiar "boys will be boys" look, and we go in after him.

Percival is just about to round a corner leading to the lights we've seen when a crackling EM voice I don't recognize startles us all. "What are you doing here?" Within seconds, we're surrounded by half a dozen stern looking electromagicians, blocking our passage forward and our escape. The tallest one has dark hair that mostly covers a long scar cutting diagonally across his forehead.

Percival is unfazed and stands tall. "What's going on here?" he asks, expecting no trouble. We're all EMs, after all. And we're steps from Torden's pavilion. Trouble between EMs here would be like Catholics getting into a fist fight at St. Peter's.

"Nothing you need to worry about," Scarface says.

Percival recoils mockingly. "That's a little terse, don't you think? I'm just asking a question, buddy."

Scarface looks to his companions briefly then back to us. With a polished smoothness, his expression lightens and he smiles. "Sorry, I didn't mean to sound abrupt. It's just that it's a little *dangerous* here. Torden has us making improvements to expand into the south wing, but you know how rickety this whole structure is." Scarface grins a conciliatory grin, but it feels strange to me.

"Oh, okay, well sorry to bother you," Percival says, turning to leave. The EMs around us relax a bit and step aside, and I figure that's that. Till Percival stops. "But why are you working on it in the middle of the night?" Startling us all, he dives between two EMs and rushes forward, toward the light.

"Somebody grab him!" Scarface blurts angrily.

There's a mad scramble of arms and bodies, people trying to get a hold on Percival. But he's lithe and athletic, and slithers past them. The EMs run after, leaving Zee and me behind. So of course we follow our friend. Whatever's going on, they don't want us there, and Percival might need our help. At the very least, I figure we might be dragged in front of Torden to explain ourselves, and Percival would need eyewitnesses that were on his side.

Turning a corner, we step into the glow of electric lamps, and see Percival frozen in shock. The EMs surrounding him block most of our view, but between their shifting bodies, I see enough.

In the south yard, chained to a wall under the glow of floodlights, a captive Stickman hisses and writhes like a nightmare come true.

PART II

STICKMEN

13

IN THE NAME OF SCIENCE

They drag us physically back into the pavilion, leading us not into Torden's large meeting hall, but instead a small chamber. Candles once again light the way, making the room feel claustrophobic with so many people stuffed into it. Torden apparently has been informed prior to our arrival, as he's standing in the center of the room with his arms crossed, looking annoyed. Rand stands slightly behind him, as always, the whispering advisor to the king. "Well, you all have been on an adventure," Torden says, attempting for some sort of humor and failing.

"What the hell is going on around here?" I say, wresting myself free of the grasp of the EM holding me. "You've got a *Stickman* captive in the yard!" I guess I expect a gasp from the assembled crowd, but of course everyone present except us already knows. Instead, I get a sort of impatient sigh.

"Lyn, there are so many things you don't understand."

"Try me," I sneer.

"Let me ask you this first," Torden says. "Who are you three to be snooping around here? What makes you think that's acceptable? What makes you think it's *your place* to do that? We have dozens of EMs here, yourselves excluded. Why do you three who seldom set foot in this place think you have the right to try to upset the balance of things here?"

"Did you not hear me, Torden?" I say, pissed off. "A Stickman. Captive. In the yard. How do explain that? And I wonder what the others here will think when we tell them?"

Torden laughs briefly, confidently. "Tell them? As if they don't already know. As I have said, you seldom come here. What do you know of our ways?"

Zee, Percival, and I exchange confused glances. Can we really be *that* out of touch? To not know about something as completely nuts as holding a Stickman?

"If they know," Zee says, "then why are we crammed in this little room rather than in the main chamber?"

Torden tilts his head and smirks, but doesn't answer. *He's lying to us. They don't really know*, I think. *Why would he lie to us?*

"Why is it here, then, Torden? Why do you have it?" I say.

"*It?*" he asks. "The Golem, I assume you mean. What you so crudely call a *Stickman*. It is here for one simple purpose — a purpose you would already know, if you lived among us. Research."

"What the hell does that mean?" Percival says.

Torden nods, thinking. "I would tell you myself, but then I believe you'd say I'm making it up. Therefore, ask anyone in the room. Anyone. Let them tell you the truth."

I scan the room, realizing only Torden and Rand are known to me. Seeing the expression on Zee's face, and Percival's, it seems they have the same problem. These EMs are strangers. Conveniently, we can pick from any number of people we know nothing about, and have no idea if we can trust. The no-win situation.

"Him," I say, pointing at probably the youngest person in the room, a wiring, dark-haired kid maybe five years younger than me. Then I pause. "Hold on, let me ask a question first. Why are there no women in here except Zee and me?" Torden feigns surprise, a look that doesn't sit well on his face. It looks like the mask of bullshit. All of a sudden, none of the men in the room want to speak. Typical. So I stab a finger again toward the guy I chose. "Whatever. Him. I pick him to tell us what's going on."

The kid's eyes dart around, looking toward everyone else quickly then falling away. He looks skittish and flustered, part of the reason why I picked him in the first place. "Um..." he starts before going silent, his eyes still flitting back and forth.

I try to look sympathetic. More than anything, I try to look like someone who's more likely to *relate* to this kid than a two hundred year old wannabe king. "Torden said you'd tell us the truth. That's all we want." I smile, willing myself to look like a friend to this stranger.

"It's... it's here for research," the kid says. "Torden wants to eradicate the Golem — um, you know, the Stickmen — for all of us. He's going to save us from them."

I squint at the kid trying to gauge if he's telling the truth, and it sure seems like he is. And Torden had told me his thoughts on how to kill one, even though he'd never seen it. So it seems... plausible. I'm still skeptical but, damn it, it makes some degree of sense. Know your enemy, I guess. I turn back to Torden. "So then, you're going to kill it, once you figure out how?"

"No," he says, shaking his head. "Of course not. This is science, Lyn. If I *kill* the subject, I might learn something in that one moment. But if I keep him alive, I can learn *everything*."

Zee interrupts. "If you caught one, you can catch more. Who needs to study them if you can just catch them one at a time and kill them?'

"Yeah," Percival adds. "What if it gets loose? Then, instead of one fewer of them, you've got a real problem. At best, you've got one right here in the middle of you all. At worst, it goes back and returns with friends."

"Do they... communicate?" I ask in shock.

Torden twists his face into a grimace. "We have no idea. See? That's how little we know — and why we need to learn more. So please, I understand your concern, all of you, and I understand your surprise. But you need to consider the big picture. We need time to study the Golem. Time to understand it." He looks at us like he's asking our permission.

Percival cracks first. "Um, I mean, I guess it isn't hurting anyone where it is..."

"Really?" I say, wheeling on him.

"I agree," Zee adds. "Even though I don't like it, maybe it's for the best." I'm about to say something harsh and disbelieving to Zee, when she adds one more thought. "Maybe if we actually *knew* something about those damn things, Robin would still be alive."

14

DEALING WITH REGULARS

I wake up back in my bed, realizing with a tinge of annoyance that it's still my safe place. My home. My room. The world of EMs and Stickmen and Torden and all that — it doesn't touch me here. As much as the ancient decor of my room ticks me off, it makes me feel warm and comfortable, too. Don't tell anyone. I'll deny it.

I nuzzle in the unassuming ease of the many layers of my covers, curling up, not waiting for something to happen. No, the opposite. Hoping nothing happens. I can stay here all day.

"Lyn?" Kevin's voice calls from below, and I know my peace is over. It's breakfast time, and Kevin holds breakfast sacred, much like the unchanging certainty of my room's decor.

"Coming," I shout before burying myself further into the blankets. For a moment, I do nothing. But the magic spell is broken, the moment caught between sleep and wake. In less than three minutes, I slough off the covers, flop my feet to the floor, and pad for the bathroom.

KEVIN SITS at the head of the long dining room table, which is more than a little bit absurd given that there's just the two of us. And it's breakfast. But Kevin is Kevin, so I just play along. He's not an ostentatious jerk, he just likes to stick to customs. Of course, Kevin is eighteen years older than me — I often wonder if I was an accident — so it makes sense that his way of thinking is a little older and more conservative than mine. I take up residence to his left side, because sitting at his right like some warlord's lieutenant seems like amateur hour. Also, it's the seat I've sat in for years. Also, I first chose it for the same reason just noted. Sometimes things don't change. I guess I have my own customs.

"Morning," he says, nodding. In his right hand, he holds the financial newspaper folded neatly to the article he's reading. With his left, he sips coffee.

"Kev," I return, knowing that he doesn't like to be called *Kev* but tolerates it from his sister. I'm wearing my typical attire, hoodie and gloves, knowing that Kevin doesn't like that either. He just doesn't know I can't answer my phone without gloves on.

"Lyn," Kevin says from somewhere behind his raised coffee and paper. "Haven't we talked about wearing gloves to the table? It's breakfast."

"They're comfortable," I say.

Juliet appears with a ready plate, placing steaming eggs before me with fresh fruit on the side. The eggs are piping hot but exquisitely cooked, another feather in her cap. She always times everything perfectly. "Coffee today?" Juliet asks.

"Please," I say, smiling.

So, do you see what I mean? How my home life was *so* much different from anything else I did? Can you imagine Percival seeing me this way? Or Torden?

Thinking of my so-called real life brings back thoughts of Robin. He's out there somewhere, still, though he isn't himself. I feel compelled to find him and end his misery, but at the same time, I can't imagine the horror of Zee witnessing that. Which makes me think I can't let her be there when it happens. I'd have to find the Stickman that was Robin and deal with it privately.

It.

I just thought of Robin as an *it.*

I drop my fork with a too loud clang and put my head in my hands. *Why Robin?*

"Lyn?" Kevin asks, looking up from his paper. "Everything okay?"

I'm near tears, but force them away. And, come on, you've probably been there, right? Really sad, then suddenly interrupted? What does that make you? It's partially because it pulls you out of whatever shell you were in, and partially the embarrassment of being caught about to cry. It makes you really mad. At least that's what it does for me. "I'm fine, don't worry about it," I say in a huff.

Kevin puts down the paper, neatly beside his plate. It's probably parallel to the knife, for all I know, because Kevin is an obnoxious perfectionist. "Hey now, don't be upset with me. What can I do to help you, Lyn?"

Oh, God. The condescension of that statement. I *know* in my heart that Kevin means well, but I *hate* when he thinks he can fix everything that goes wrong with me. "Nothing. Really. Drop it, okay?" *And,* I think, *my name is Lightning.* But I never, ever would use that name with my brother. No way. He wouldn't understand why I chose such a name. He could never understand the life of an EM.

I reach for a second copy of the paper — yes, of course we get a copy for each of us, even though I probably haven't glanced at the financial news in more than two years. Brusquely flipping through pages, I find the first mildly interesting article — believe me, even that's a stretch — and hold the paper in front of my face like a shield between me and my brother.

Kevin pushes back in his chair, and I instantly know how this conversation will end. Kevin has his teeth sunk into it, and I don't want that. An argument is inevitable. Juliet suddenly pretends there's something pressing to check on in the kitchen, and she leaves the room. Not for the first time, I wish I could disappear like her. "Really, Lyn. You can talk to me. I don't bite." He smiles.

Fine, I think. *I'll try.* "A friend of mine. He died."

Kevin leans forward with concern. "Oh my God, Lyn, who? Not Mackenzie?"

I wave my hands and shake my head. "No, no... not Zee. I guy. You don't know him. His name was Robin."

"Was he...?" Kevin's tone makes it clear what he means.

"No, God, no! Just because I mentioned a guy's name doesn't mean I was dating him. He was just a friend."

"Sorry, sorry, Lyn." Kevin is flustered, but gets back on topic quickly. "What happened?"

I'm silent. You know, because telling him the truth would be a little... *odd*. Wouldn't it?

"Lyn? What happened to your friend, Robin?" Kevin's tone is calm, but probing. Oddly, it's almost like one of those detective shows, where the detective already knows what he wants you to say, but he asks his questions anyway to hear the answers from your mouth.

Now I'm completely regretting saying anything, because telling the truth is impossible, and lying about Robin's death seems cruel and horrible. "It was sudden, unexpected. I — I don't know." Not a lie, not the full truth. My face is flushed red. I feel hot and strange and on the edge where tears might come.

Kevin nods thoughtfully. "I see. What do you need?"

I crinkle up my face. "What?"

Once more, Kevin leans forward, this time putting his hand on my arm. "Lyn, I'm your brother. Let me help. What can I do for you and your friend? Are funeral services needed? Are there any medical bills? I can help with those, if not."

And that, friends and neighbors, *that* pisses me off. Because Robin will never need a funeral service. He's a walking, charred electro monster. "No, definitely not. No."

"His family? Do they need anything? Help with costs?" Kevin is trying hard to look like the earnest, concerned friend and brother, but damn, he's making me mad.

"Kev, look. I get it. You have a lot of money. You can buy almost anything. But not everything can be solved with money. This certainly can't." I push back from the table, having eaten maybe a third of what Juliet provided.

"*I* have a lot of money?" he says, in an almost comically insulted way. "Lyn, *we* have a lot of money. You included. Sure, Mom and Dad said in their will that they wanted me to manage the estate, but it's *ours*. Which is why helping you, helping your friend — that's something we both can be happy to support." And if he had left it there, I might not have blown up at him. "It's certainly much better than those frivolous trips you take on my credit card."

I stand up, angry. "They aren't frivolous. How would you know anyway? Do you know *anything* about my life? My *real* life? No, of course not. You're too busy with your nose in the financial news." I take my copy of the paper and fling it across the table. It opens midair and sections of paper fluttering into heaps, some falling to the floor. I storm off for my room, realizing at the same time how our differences so easily piss me off, and how silly our arguments can be. He's just a regular person after all, and sometimes, in addition to normal sibling issues, dealing with regulars can be too much. But he deserved it this time, right? Maybe not? Ah, be quiet.

———

IN MY ROOM ONCE AGAIN, I tap my phone with a gloved hand. Seconds before I push the button to dial Zee, I realize she's had it the hardest. I decide to leave her be and dial Percival instead.

"Good morning, Lyn," he says, answering.

"Lightning," I say out of habit.

"Lightning, sorry. What's up?"

"How can we find one?" I say. "How can we bring it out of hiding? And where do they live? How can we trap one like Torden?"

Percival is flustered. "Whoa, slow down. What are you talking about?"

"A Stickman. I want to figure out how to kill one, and I want you to help me." I say it forcefully. It's not a question.

Percival sighs dramatically, but I think he sounds excited by the idea. "I'm going to need to call in sick, then."

"Oh please," I say. "You don't have a job."

"Yeah, but I do have *jobs*."

"Do I want to know?" I ask. Ah, Percival's many rumored jobs.

"Probably not," he says.

"Fine. Call them, whoever they are, and tell them you're sick. Then meet me in a half an hour."

15

THE HUNT BEGINS

A while later, we're wandering the streets up where the last impromptu Fuse Box happened, mostly because we don't have any better idea of where to look for rogue Stickmen.

"When one jumps out at us, then what?" Percival says.

"We kill it," I say, seriously. Percival doesn't reply, but I feel the heat of his stare on the side of my face. He thinks I'm crazy.

The whole process feels silly and random, with us just circling blocks around where the attack occurred, seeing if our mere presence stirs up trouble. An hour and a half later, we have no answers, no sightings, and the only surprise we've stumbled into is how boring it can be to hunt for Stickmen.

"How long do you want to do this?" Percival asks, checking his watch.

"Until it works."

He nods. "So that might be a while, it seems."

"Do you have any better ideas?"

"Nope."

We keep walking, sweeping block after block, expanding outward in a pattern that seems to be taking us further and further away from anything like a ghost of chance.

———

WE GIVE up less than twenty minutes later, on the pretense of needing a short break and a snack. Percival and I pop into a cafe on West 110th Street where we each grab a cold drink and order a panini to split, then we walk over to the northwest corner of Central Park to find a spot to eat. We end up on the steps of Blockhouse No. 1, which reminds me of miniature version of the tower at Garrett Mountain Park in Jersey. You know, the place where Percival kissed me. So that's on my mind as we share our lunch. "Thanks," I say between bites. The cafe cut our panini in two, so we each have our distinct half. Percival's is nearly gone, while mine is less than half eaten.

"For the sandwich?" he asks. "But you bought it."

"For coming out here with me," I say, not even chiding him for his failure to understand.

"Oh yeah, sure," he says. "I had nothing going on anyway."

"I thought you had jobs to do."

Percival smiles. "Well, yeah, I did."

"And you cancelled them to help me. So thanks."

"I cancelled them to spend time with you," he says. Just like that. Nothing else. Just plain and obvious. I'm flustered and can't think of what to say in response. So I drop my eyes toward the ground and take another bite. Still, every ounce of my focus is on him in my peripheral vision. His blond hair wavers slightly in the breeze, and his perfect teeth seem to glint in the sun as he takes the last bite of his half of the sandwich.

People pass by almost constantly, in groups or individually. It's midday in Central Park, and it's busy, so being alone in the park isn't the risk it would be at night. Percival seems content to people watch as I finish my food. But I realize he's fixated, looking at one particular person for a long time. "Something wrong?" I ask after my panini has disappeared and I'm crumpling up the wrapper.

"Nah, just weird."

"What's weird?"

Percival points, which seems like it would be tremendously rude. "You see that guy?"

I follow the tip of his finger to find a man sprawled out in the grass beneath a tree. He isn't moving. "Someone's having a nap," I say.

"Well, a chemically induced one, at least," Percival says. Other people, families with kids, joggers, people in business attire taking a break, they all walk by. No one stops or really even registers the guy passed out nearby.

"What do you expect in the city?" I say, because honestly, what do you expect? You can run into a junkie pretty much anywhere.

"It just has me wondering," Percival says.

"Care to share, or are you just going to leave me in the dark?"

"We all know about the junkies," he says.

"Of course. There are junkies all over the place."

"No, I mean the *junkies*. EM junkies."

"Oh," I say. "*Those* junkies. Yeah." It was a topic every EM knew about but few discussed. A percentage of people who discover that they can wield electromagic end up getting addicted to the charge, in the worst possible way. When you get your power the natural way, from lightning, from storms, that's one thing. But if you *have to have it*, you can't wait around for a storm to brew up. Those people can end up as junkies. "What about them?"

"What is an EM junkie, anyway?" Percival asks rhetorically, clearly about to mansplain something to me. I decide to allow it for a moment, as long as the lecture doesn't go on too long. "An EM junkie is just someone who has to have power all the time, or at least as much as possible."

"Uh huh," I say, not following why this is suddenly relevant. Or why I need it spelled out to me when I already know it.

"Okay, then, what is a Stickman?"

"Nothing. Us. A shell of us."

"Right," Percival says emphatically, turning toward me and putting one hand on my knee in a way that doesn't distract me at all, really. I swear. Shut up. "They're like us, but what do they do? They suck up all the power."

"You're right, but I'm not following how this helps us. How do we find one? We've been circling around for hours."

Percival leans in and now his face fills my vision, his nose just inches from mine. "What if Stickmen are like EM junkies? What if they have to be around power all the time?"

Immediately, I get his point. I smile. "Then we'll find Stickmen in the same place we'd find a junkie."

"The power plant," he says, returning my smile.

I turn my head to the side. "You know what, *farm boy*?"

"What, *Lyn*?" he says, almost whispering in my ear.

"That's a really good idea," I say, turning back and leaning in until my lips meet his. The first time in my life I ever initiate a kiss. Percival's hands rise and hold each side of my face, gently.

It's a while before we decide to leave the park, hand in hand. It's a good thing no one I know is watching, because otherwise I think I'd die of embarrassment.

———

"WELL, LOOKEE HERE," Percival says in dramatic fashion.

"Don't," I say, too serious. A black sedan from my family's car service has pulled over to pick us up just outside the park. "Just... *don't*."

His tone changes to a defensive one. "Sorry, it's just, you know, not my typical ride."

I roll my eyes, opening the door and holding it for him. *Chivalry*, I think, *is woefully outdated bullshit*. "Get in."

"Afternoon, Ms. Hopkins," the driver says. It's William, and that's a good thing. After Harry, he knows me best. Knows I don't like chit chat. "Sir," he says to Percival with a nod. A moment later, the car slides out into traffic, making its way along the edge of Central Park, heading downtown. I give our destination as a restaurant in the East Village, which is strange since we just ate, but William doesn't know that. There's traffic, of course. And a parade we have to skirt around. It's midday in the city. Shocker. Thirty minutes to go just a few miles.

William ends up taking us south along the East River, and we drive directly past the power plant before turning right and driving a couple blocks farther. Seeing the plant go by makes me shudder. Percival and I will end up walking back, but that's for the best. Not sure if the car service drivers actually *care* where they drop me off, but there's no reason to make it look overly suspicious.

"Do you want me to stay close, ma'am, for the return trip?" William asks, looking at me in the rearview.

I almost say no, but something overrules that, despite the fact that I'm not keen on Percival seeing this side of me. "We'll be a little while, so you don't have to, you know, idle outside or anything. But if you could be available for us, I'd appreciate it."

"Yes, ma'am. Enjoy your meal," he says with a nod.

Once Percival and I get out, William pulls away, turns a corner, and is gone.

Percival looks at the restaurant, a noodle shop of no particular merit or renown. "Hungry?" he asks.

"Nope," I say, turning and walking toward the river a few blocks distant. "Come on."

We don't talk as we walk down East 14th Street, the smokestacks of the power plant like a beacon drawing us onward, ominously dominating the skyline at the far end of the street. How is it we know where to go? Simple. Every EM knows the power plant. It's central to every morality play we electromagicians pass on to one another. When you're a newb, you get the not-too-subtle warnings: *Don't end up like the junkies at the power plant! Heed my words! Beware!* Real dramatic stuff like that. Which is why it's now remarkably weird to be walking toward those smokestacks on purpose.

The building is fairly nondescript red brick, but with the smokestacks jutting out the top, a mass of pipes, tubes, and girders adorning the front, and a side yard overloaded with those conical electrical zapper thingees — that's a technical term, sorry — it all looks like something from a steampunk movie or possibly the overblown laboratory for a mad scientist.

"Ready?" Percival asks, breaking the silence.

"Sure," I say. "I just wish I knew what I was ready *for*."

"I was thinking the same thing."

We cross the street to stand just outside the blue metal gate of the power plant, realizing how much that might be a problem. Other than circling a several block radius, there might not be much to see unless we can get inside the gate. And that, of course, would be the quickest way to get ourselves arrested. Besides electrical-grid terrorists, who's gonna break into the power plant? So we start by circling, trying to figure out how to get ourselves inside the perimeter wall.

On the south side of the campus, we follow the fence line east toward the water. It occurs to me for about the millionth time that we disrespect our waterfronts in the city. We build highways along them, do our best to ignore them. Other places cherish the water's edge as their most valuable real estate. In New York, we do things like putting a bank of dumpsters closest to the river. That's where Percival and I end up, and the smell is heavenly. In that it stinks to high heaven, I mean. The odor is physically oppressive, threatening to knock us out, so when Percival makes a suggestion, I'm quick to accept it. "What do you say we lift ourselves over this fence and see what's happening inside?" he asks.

I hold my nose and reach inside for electromagic. It operates strangely here, so close to so much electricity. It's somewhat like paddling a canoe in the middle of a tsunami, but it works. Checking quickly that no one is nearby, I lift my feet off the ground and loop over, landing in a back corner of the power plant's side yard.

No more than ten feet from me, an EM junkie is curled in a ball, lying on the ground by the fence. Though I touch down without a sound, his eyes suddenly snap open and he looks right at me, like the energy flowing through me is calling to him, moth to the flame.

16

POWER SOURCES

Percival lands next to me, and both of us snuff out our electromagic. Still, the EM junkie stares at us. Is he confused, threatened? Or does he want to harm us?

"Is that Gregg?" Percival asks in a whisper.

I look closer. With the junkies, it's hard to tell. First, they spend no time on their appearance, so their hair is usually wild, clothes usually dirty and torn. Second, consuming power all the time does something to them, aging them in a strange way that makes them look both ancient and forever impossibly young. It's like bad plastic surgery, where you understand the end product is supposed to make the person look youthful, but you can see all too well the tinges of age in every fold of skin. "Maybe?" I say.

Around us, arrays of metal pipes and conduits are like massive spiders or octopi, their arms reaching in every direction over our heads. The thrum of power — of electricity, our specific kind of power — emanates from every direction. Percival steps in front of me, putting himself between me and what may be Gregg Magdeburg, an EM we knew from years past, now a junkie. He also has more Gs in his name than your average person, not that that's a typical measure of a person's merit.

I appreciate that Percival is willing to step up like that, stand between me and danger, but of course I bristle at the insinuation that I can't handle things myself. Nonetheless, Gregg the junkie's focus wanes and he lets his head fall back down. In moments, his eyes are closed.

"That was interesting," Percival says. "So what if our theory is right and we *do* find Stickmen here? Aren't you afraid?"

"Yes," I say. "Terrified. But this is just recon."

"What's that supposed to mean?"

"If we find a Stickman," I say, "we leave, quickly. We get reinforcements and come back."

Percival nods but looks unsure. "Who?"

"Zee, of course. And maybe Hayden? And..." I trail off because I can't think of any other EM who might help us, especially if it even remotely seemed like defiance of Torden. I realize at this moment how much of a strangle hold Torden actually has over us, and that makes me both angry as hell and deeply sad.

Percival must notice the change in my mood, and he takes my hand, giving it a little squeeze. "It's enough. Whether it's four of us, or three, or even just me and you, it's enough." He says it so convincingly, I almost believe him. "But there are others. Mary Tate. Walter. Maybe Uma and Zeb. I don't believe for a minute that every EM in the pavilion is Torden's lap dog."

"I hope not," I say. "Come on. Let's actually look around before we get arrested just for standing here." I lead Percival gingerly past the sleeping junkie and turn behind one of the massive metal structures, weaving our way through the yard. In fewer than twenty yards, we come across another sleeping EM junkie, this one still tapped into a power source — he's holding on to one of the smaller pine cone shaped elements connected to the grid around us. I don't even want to touch him, for fear of accidentally connecting myself to the massive pool of man-made electricity around us.

Because that's the problem: man-made. For whatever reason, it just isn't the same as the real deal, the natural kind. I'm sure that some scientist would refute what I'm saying, tell me that all electricity is the same, but I can promise you it's not. Every EM has tried man-made electricity — from a wall socket, wherever — at some point in her life. It leaves a horrible taste in the back of your mouth, I think. Others say it upsets their stomach, or gives them a massive headache. But a small percentage of EMs like it, get addicted to it. They can't get enough of the power, and it's everywhere around them. They waste their days jacked into sockets, and then when that's not good enough, they go directly to circuit breaker boards. Eventually none of that's enough, and they end up living like vagrants at the power plant. Of course they get busted, all the time. But regulars just think they're homeless or drunk. They don't know why certain people keep breaking into the power plant and are found asleep in some back corner like the two we run into. The regular people don't know they're there for the juice.

Just before I turn the next corner, past yet another massive set of pipes and girders, I hear a sound like a grunt, and I figure we've stumbled into a third EM junkie. But something in the sound warns me. Junkies are passive, pathetic. The sound we hear seems, I don't know... *earnest.* Or maybe eager is the better word.

I come around the bend to find myself almost face to face with a Stickman, here in broad daylight. In one millisecond, I think, *Wow, we were right.* In the next, I shout, "Run!"

What saves us, I believe, in that instance, is the structure all around us, humming with energy. I've never known a Stickman to be thoughtful, but this one seems perplexed. Something about the power plant has it in an oddly conflicted mood. I don't care. I just turn, push Percival, and we race back the way we came.

Once he gets going, Percival is quick, rounding corners and dodging pipes. We reach the first of the EM junkies, the one still jacked in, and Percival just leaps over his prone body. Moments later, I do the same.

We're about to turn another corner, when a horrifying idea strikes me. *We just left that EM to die!* I stop. I turn.

The Stickman barges into the space and now it's one on one. Me and him. The Stickman looks at me with its charred, evil face, then I watch as it clearly turns its attention downward.

"No!" I say. Percival must have noticed I stopped, and hears my cry. He returns to stand beside me. To face off with a Stickman. If I wasn't terrified and about to burst forth with as much electromagic power as I can muster, I would kiss him. The Stickman approaches the sleeping junkie slowly, slithering like a snake, low to the ground. "Leave him alone!"

The Stickman ignores me, and I hesitate. It hovers over the junkie, reminding me of vampire movies where the regal count in the black and red cape would dramatically lunge down upon the neck of the hapless maiden. Not here, though. The blackened form of the Stickman lingers above the completely oblivious EM junkie, and then... turns away.

He doesn't want that *kind of power*, I think, before realizing what that really means. *He wants ours.* "Oh shit!" Once more, I push Percival and he wordlessly understands. It's time to go. We dash by the second EM junkie until we reach a part of the yard with relatively open skies, where none of the giant electrical grids block our upward escape.

It's a rule among EMs never to use your ability to hover, float, or fly in the daytime — too easy for regulars to see you and then what would we have? For hundreds of years, EMs have lived invisibly among the regulars, but today is not the day for rules. Now is not the time to worry about exposure, when there's a Stickman on our asses. "Let's go!" I shout to Percival and we both glow blue with energy, zipping up and away from the yard. We go further, higher, until we arc over the entire power plant building. I hope, if anyone sees it, they think it's just a pair of errant electrical sparks. Human sized, of course.

We don't look back, dropping ourselves down on the far side of the plant and trying to quickly scan in all directions. Miraculously, it doesn't seem like anyone notices us. Across the street there are baseball fields, and on one of them a game is underway. We hurry along the tree lined sidewalk next to the field and I grab for my phone, tapping one of my auto-dial options. In seconds, William answers. "Ready for a pickup now, ma'am?"

"Yes, definitely," I say, out of breath. I mention the baseball field and ask him to meet us on the north side, hoping the Stickman gave up chasing us when we disappeared so quickly.

William is a pro, and he glides up only two or three minutes later. Despite my urging, it seems he was simply waiting somewhere nearby. Still looking over our shoulders, we both jump in the car. William notices our heavy breathing and the sweat beading on our foreheads. "You all look like you've had a workout — everything okay?"

I glance at Percival sideways and smile. "Yeah, um, it was just a... really exciting baseball game."

17

THE HIGH ORDER

"Where to, ma'am?" William asks.

I almost say *home*, but I realize we have work to do. "8th and West 36th, please."

"Your friend Mackenzie's?"

I smile. "You have a very good memory, William."

He nods at me in the rear view and returns to driving without another word. Like I said, he's a pro.

Twenty minutes or so later — enough time for my heart rate to return to normal — William is slipping into an opening directly in front of Zee's building, even though I didn't give him the specific address. "Shall I wait again, ma'am?" he asks, but I decline. Where we go next, we'll need anonymous transportation. William pulls away with a polite wave.

"You didn't pay him," Percival says, confused. "Or tip him, or anything."

"My brother pays for things. I don't have any money," I say over my shoulder as I walk up to the building, using a tone that makes it clear I don't want to discuss the topic further. It's a lie I tell too often, that I don't have money, to avoid the bullshit that comes with people expecting you to have deep pockets.

Zee buzzes us in and we climb the stairs to her apartment. In short order, she hears what happened at the power plant. "We need to tell Torden. If there's one Stickman, there could be others. We're going to need everyone working together. Maybe his experiments will help us catch or destroy it—" Then she catches herself. "Was it...?"

"No," I say quickly. "Pretty sure it wasn't." *Robin.*

"Pretty sure?" she asks, trembling.

"It wasn't him," Percival says, in a firm and reassuring voice. "I'm positive. I saw the Stickman better than Lyn, and I can say for sure it wasn't him." I don't know if Percival is telling the truth or just trying to save Zee's feelings, and honestly it doesn't matter. For years, Percival has been a guy I knew of questionable morals and intelligence. All the sudden, in the space of just a few days, he seems to be hitting all the right notes. I hope it isn't a passing phase.

"Well, this *has* to make Torden listen," Zee says emphatically. "If you all can find a Stickman, maybe we can work with Torden and the rest to eliminate them all, once and for all."

I share a look with Percival, and it isn't a hopeful one. "He said he wanted to keep it alive, the one he had. If we tell him where to find more, what will he do then?"

"Yeah," Percival says. "Maybe start a zoo." It's a joke, and not funny. I should have known the old Percival was still in there. Wishful thinking.

"Sure," Zee says, "but Torden is the best we have — especially if he's been studying them. We have to go tell him what you found. He can keep his captive one for study, but he'll have to see the sense in getting rid of the rest of them." Zee freezes. "Oh my God."

I put a hand on her arm, calming her, though have no idea what's suddenly wrong. "Zee, what?"

She looks a me, eyes like saucers. "What if there's like a *den* or something? I mean, what if there are *a lot* of Stickmen at the power plant?"

It was definitely possible, given what we'd seen, finding them just where we thought we might. And here Percival and I walked in like a couple taking a stroll in Central Park. What if we'd encountered ten instead of one? Could there possibly *be* ten Stickmen in the city? The idea makes me shudder involuntarily. "Zee's right. There could be more. We'll need everyone's help — and especially Torden's knowledge — if we want to fix this. If we want to get rid of them."

Percival nods. "Well that's two in favor, so I guess my vote doesn't count."

I smirk back at him. "Sure it counts, farm boy. It just doesn't *change* anything. So, grab us a cab, will you?"

———

BEING the middle of the day, it isn't strictly illegal to go Orchard Beach the way it is at night, so we just have the cabbie drop us off in the parking lot. We talk like we're going to hang out by the water, then make our way to the north side once the car with its flat yellow-orange color disappears through the trees.

We cut to our left and find our way toward Torden's front door.

Stop where you are, a voice says to us, crackling with static.

We freeze. "It's us," I say. "We were just here."

We know who you are, the voice says in an unfriendly tone. *Turn around and leave. Now.*

A second voice joins the conversation, and we see their sources — EMs high up on the walls, looking down on us with disdain. *Run along home, scum.* A ruddy faced twenty-something with curls of red hair scowls at us.

"*Scum*?" I say out loud. "Really? What the hell is going on here? Have you all lost your minds?"

The redhead glances to his left and smiles. *Hardly,* he says. *Maybe we've finally come to our senses. About you all.* The other guard, also in his twenties, but dark haired and built like he was carved from stone, grins back.

"Open the door," Percival says. "We have important news."

They laugh. "Opening the door is one thing we will *not* be doing for you, ever again."

Zee broadcasts her voice, and I realize she's trying to play peace broker, making sure her words are silent, in the tradition of EMs visiting the pavilion. "Please. This is important. I don't know what you all have been told about us, but our friend was taken by a Stickman. We have news that might help all of us get rid of Stickmen forever! Help us all get those things out of our city."

"So the thief has a voice," the redhead says, eliciting another laugh from the blockier guard.

"Thief?" I say aloud. "What are you talking about?"

Dark-hair squints at me. "Your friend stole important documents from Torden when she was last here. If that's news to you, sorry to hear it. But the fact is, all three of you are banned. By decree of the High Order."

Banned? I thought. The word sank ominously, like a heavy stone thrown in a lake. I look at Zee, and she returns the look, baffled. *She didn't steal squat. This is all a bunch of lies. But why? Hold on... this is about what we found. They're banning us for finding the Stickman.* I broadcast my voice to the guards. "Did your precious Torden tell you about the Stickman he has locked up maybe 100 yards over that way?" I smile, thinking I've just dropped a truth bomb on them.

"Of course," the dark-haired one says. "Everyone here knows all about that. Torden is working under the explicit direction of the entire High Order."

"What is this High Order you keep mentioning?" I ask.

Again, they laugh. Man, being a guard is a chuckle a minute, it seems. They don't answer. To one side, I feel Zee looking at me. "What?" I say.

Zee whispers. "Torden is one of our elders, called the High Order. Do you really not know this?"

"Nope," I say. "I've made it my habit to avoid this place, and avoid the people inside. Do you really not know that?"

Zee shrugs and Percival grimaces. "Any city that has a population of EMs is run by an elder, a member of the High Order."

I think for minute. "What about Rand, Torden's little sidekick? Is he High Order, too?"

Percival answers. "No, he's a level lower, just called the Order. You really never heard this stuff before, Lyn? We've heard it since we were kids..."

Zee trails off. She knows what my childhood was like, losing both parents. I scowl. Worse, now I feel completely ostracized. The EMs high above us are laughing, protecting some hierarchy of power that I never heard of before, or never bothered to learn about. And my friends are scoffing at my ignorance. *Shit.* I start to walk away, annoyed with everyone, myself most of all.

"Yeah, run off, *Lightning*," the redhead calls mockingly. "Maybe some other group will take you in. DC, Chicago. Hell, maybe you'll need to go all the way to Tokyo or Paris. Nah, for you... try Sydney. I hear they like the weirdos like you."

I wheel around, suddenly full of my electromagic. "Why don't you just shut your mouth before I shut it for you?" I'm glowing with energy, but it's futile. An EM attacking an EM is just a gift. *Here, have some of my power.* Another EM would be happy to get zapped by my electricity — I'd probably save them the effort of standing in the rain during the next storm.

Above me, all I hear is laughter as I head back toward the parking lot, already using my phone to call a cab.

18

VIVA LA REVOLUTION

"They can all go to hell," I say, pacing back and forth in the parking lot, wondering why the cab is taking so long.

"Those guys were jerks," Percival says, trying to placate me.

I freeze. "I don't mean just those guys, I mean *every* EM. They can *all* go to hell." Then I realize my blunder. "Except you two." Shit. Everything is a mess. I can't even be angry right.

Zee looks like she's seen a ghost, but I'm too pissed to really notice. Not yet.

Percival seems like he's grasping at straws. "There are others, like us. There have to be. Maybe in another city."

I get in his face. It's not his fault, nothing is, but anger is anger and has to be released. "I'm not moving to some other city because of *those* people. I was born here. My *parents* were born here."

Percival looks at me with something like disappointment, and I realize all too well that I am the privileged one. The one with the big house. Zee has a tiny apartment. Percival lives in a basement in Jersey. "Maybe the rest of us aren't so attached to this place as you," he says.

I'm an ass, I think.

"This is all such *bullshit*," Zee says. "Torden, Stickmen... *Robin*. I have a job here — I can't just fly away. Being an EM doesn't pay jack shit. Even if I left, what if they tell others, in other cities, to shun us, too? I'm ostracized. For life. It's not like dating a *regular* person is even an option, right?"

I suddenly understand. With Robin gone, and with no access to other EMs, Zee could be single until she dies. I mean, she could try to date regulars, but eventually, hiding what you are all the time... it doesn't really work for us. Somehow my mom pulled it off, married to my dad, a regular. But they were by far the exception. I glance at Percival and he returns my look, like we're acknowledging how lucky we are. At least we got kicked out together.

"I need to think," Zee says, storming off toward the turnstiles that guard entrance to the lot. Did she catch our shared glance? Did she understand it? I want to think no, but I bet she did.

There's an awkward silence between Percival and me, and I know I need to be the one to break it. "Sorry," I say.

"For what?" he replies, though his tone makes it clear he wants the apology.

"For forgetting what a spoiled rich kid I am sometimes. For assuming something I think or believe or can do is the same thing for you, or for Zee."

"You'd have to apologize directly to her," he says. "I don't know what she's thinking right now."

I take a step toward Percival. "Okay, then, just you. Can you forgive me? I only meant that these guys — Torden's EMs — are wrong and we're right. And we shouldn't get kicked to the curb by their lies."

"I agree with you there," Percival says. Still, he seems reserved.

I take another step forward, and now I'm right in front of him, looking up into his eyes. "Maybe we rebel. Fight this rather than just let it happen to us. Maybe we can go to another city — all three of us — and tell them the truth. Then, we can either get them to help us back into the community here, or maybe join theirs."

"Maybe."

I take one of Percival's hands in mind and squeeze. "Listen, I don't have all the answers. I'm just trying."

"I know," he says, eyes flicking to mine. Then he leans down and kisses me, and it's not just the fact that it's right there in public, middle of the day. We're in plain sight of Zee. I guess it means we're officially dating. After the kiss, I fall into his embrace.

Zee shouts from across the parking lot. "Car's here. Come on, lovebirds."

19

INTRUDER

Hours later, I'm at home. Juliet could use the intercom to tell me dinner's ready, but she knows I hate that old school system. A long time ago, I showed her how to text. Now, her face pops up on my phone above a simple message.

Soup's on.

We're not having soup, of course, but Juliet hangs on to this phrase because it was the one my father used to say, back when I was little and he'd call me down for supper. How many times had I run to the dining room only to discover we were eating pasta or fish, then, disappointed, asked my dad, "Where's the soup?" He'd always laugh.

I realize I'm falling into a well of emotion, missing my father. My mother, too. *Gah! Not now*, I think, rubbing my eyes and heading downstairs.

But I'm in a funk when I sit at the table, once more to my brother's left. Juliet smoothly places a plate in front of me and a bowl of salad to the side. Most of what she gives me matches what Kevin is served, but Juliet knows me and she omits the tomatoes from my salad. Bless her. I can't *stand* tomatoes. When that gooey stuff bursts out... No. Just no. Who can eat that and not gag? Oh, you like them? Good news, then. You can have mine.

"Kev," I say, not looking up. "Sorry about before."

He puts down his fork. "It's nothing, Lyn. You didn't offend me. Your friend died. I... I understand."

"I know you meant well. You were trying to help."

Kevin leans in with a concerned look. "And I meant it, too. If you, or your friend's family, needs something, please tell me."

"Thanks," I say. "But it's fine. There's nothing. I mean, at least financially. Money won't help here." Above us, the massive lead crystal chandelier weighs on me like guilt.

He nods. He pauses a moment. Then he changes the subject. "I'm headed out tonight, Lyn. I'll be gone at least a day, maybe two."

"Where?"

"Business," he says, not really answering the question.

"Business where?" I ask.

Kevin pauses, then snaps like someone coming out of a trance. "Los Angeles. Meeting some people downtown there, people coming in from a few different countries. New York is usually central enough for my meetings, but a couple of these people are from Japan, Southeast Asia, so LA makes things a lot closer for them." Kevin smiles. "It's the usual boring stuff."

After dinner, Kevin relaxes at the bar. Yeah, we have a bar. It's sort of the focal point of the house for entertainment, at the mid point of the stairs, just outside the dining room. Juliet has fixed him a gin and tonic, which he idly sips while reading a book. I hover nearby, not sure exactly why I'm doing it, until there's a buzz and we faintly hear the door open downstairs. Juliet says something muffled and the door closes. The intercom makes a fuzzy sound, then Juliet's voice comes on. "Whenever you're ready, sir, the driver is here."

"Thank you, Juliet," Kevin says, not looking up from the book. After a moment, my brother stands, takes a last sip of his drink and deposits the glass on the thick marble bar top. Then he casually heads for the stairs.

I interrupt him. "Have a good trip," I say. "I hope your, um, business is good."

Kevin smiles. "Thanks, Lyn. See you in a day or two." He gives me a look that I think it supposed to be empathy, like he has any idea what's going on in my life. I appreciate, but man. He has no clue.

Moments later the upper floors of the house are mine alone, and like so many times before, I retreat to my room. Sometimes the house is too big and too empty.

————

I'm in bed reading a book when I notice the patter of rain on my window. I look up with a degree of hope — catching some lightning on my own rooftop is a rare treat. In fact, it's only happened once. Too many taller buildings around me, though I do tend to act as my own sort of lightning rod. But no, the leaves just outside my window sway rhythmically, in that way that tells me this will be far too gentle of a storm for picking up any energy. Not that it's surprising. If there was going to be a thunderstorm in the city, I'm sure Percival or Zee would have mentioned it, and even if they didn't, my weather app is meticulously configured to keep me informed. I've seen Juliet raise her eyebrows more than once at the amount of weather alerts I get.

A rain like this feels wrong to me. Just everything getting all wet and messy, no real energy. In fact, it seems to do the opposite of a thunderstorm, draining me of power rather than filling me up. *A soaking rain*, my mother used to call it. *Good for the plants.* Thinking of her makes me melancholy again. *Yeah, but not so good for me and you, Mom.* I wish she was here. She would understand. She was the only one I could really tell everything, because we shared this weird EM thing. I know. I haven't mentioned that much. It's a hard subject for me, given that she's gone. Just disappeared one day, along with Dad. I know EMs can be killed like anybody else, so I realize they could have fallen victim to any number of accidents, been involved in some kind of unsolved crime. But nobody ever found them. They were just gone, without a trace. That's what makes me believe it had to do with power. That my mom being an EM got her and my dad killed.

I wish I could talk to her again, tell her all the crazy things going on. Maybe she could make sense of it. With her face painted across the inside of my eyelids, I fall asleep.

A DEEP THUD from above wakes me. In my groggy state, I assume it's Kevin banging around in his room late at night. He's the only one who uses the top floor these days, except for Juliet doing her cleaning. Given the time, it's not her. And with Kevin living in the master suite, I rarely ever go to the rooftop terrace, since it feels like an extension of his space. A second thud, much lighter but definitely there, stirs me further awake.

Kevin isn't home. Juliet's definitely asleep. What's making noise upstairs? I remember the rain, and hear it still performing its delicate tap dance on my window. *Maybe something blew over on the terrace.* Still, I try to focus all my senses upward. And I hear a distinct and familiar sound.

Click.

That's the terrace door, I think. *Is someone breaking into my house?* Immediately, I summon my electromagic power, creating a surreal pale blue glow in my room. *That's not going to be a great idea, buddy.* Of course, I don't need to be the protector of the house. We live in a mansion in the city, for Pete's sake. We have a security system, and I have no doubt that Juliet set it before she went to bed. Right now, a silent alarm is alerting our company, and in seconds, one of the private security guards who works for people like my brother will be heading to our house.

Still, whoever's upstairs is in the house *now*. I hear a new thud and something drops to the floor. The person is clearly not familiar with the layout of my brother's suite.

Wait, I think. *What if it isn't a person? Or at least, isn't anymore?*

Could a Stickman track me back to my house? I shudder just having the thought.

I tense myself into a sitting position, still buried under the covers, pulling even more power into myself. I hear footsteps. It sounds like someone methodically searching, going into each room. Not a raging monster.

No way. No Stickman would walk like that. They'd just blast down the stairs.

There's a faint creak and I know from years of experience that it's one of the steps between floors, about half way. Whoever was upstairs is now coming down.

I slip out of bed silently, still brimming with power. Sliding my feet to avoid making a sound, I head for my bedroom door and reach out. It's all timing now. The stairs coming down lead to the hallway just outside. Inhaling a sharp breath, I twist the handle and throw open my door, and there he is — the intruder — just leaving the stairs and entering the hall.

I bark a short cry and throw a bolt of electromagic directly into his chest. He lets loose and involuntary *oof* and is sent crashing backwards toward the bottom of the stairs, where he lands in a heap. My attack should have been enough to render him useless for a little while, but not enough to kill the man — sort of like my own built-in taser.

It's dark in the hallway but I'm still glowing. For a moment, I hope that whoever I just knocked out didn't get a clear enough look at me to tell the cops about the weird glowing woman when they cart him away. Then the guy scrambles to stand up, in a manic way.

What the hell? I think. *He should have been out for a while.*

I ready myself for another blast, but something about the shape of the man is familiar... His build, his hair...

"Percival?" I shout, rushing toward him. Of course. My bolt of energy might knock another EM back, but in the end it just transfers some of my power to him. He isn't hurt at all.

Then I get a better look at his appearance. This is Percival, Mr. Perfect. But now, he's soaking wet and looks like he's seen a ghost. "Lyn!" he says, eyes wild. He reaches out and grabs me by the shoulders, pulling our faces together. He looks crazy, and I realize I'm frightened.

"Percival — what are you doing here? What's happened to you?"

He sucks in a deep breath, and then says words that change both our lives forever. Words that make me realize my first impressions were true. He *has* seen a ghost. "Lyn, one came to my house and almost got me — a Stickman! And... I think it was Robin."

20

COME TOGETHER

The elevator door opens and a man steps out — no one I know, but he wears the white shirt, badge, and pseudo-police duty belt that easily identifies him as private security. In other words, someone Kevin pays. He has both hands on a 9mm handgun, though the barrel is pointing carefully downward. He's sees Percival and me, just sitting on the hallway floor. The lights are on now, which I'm glad I had the sense to do. In the dark, maybe the guard's gun would have been pointed forward. "Ma'am?" the guard says. "Everything okay here?" Behind him, I see Juliet, still hovering in the elevator, a concerned look on her face.

"Yes," I say with a sigh. "Sorry — sorry about the trouble. It's nothing. My friend must have tripped the alarm." Percival gives a sheepish grin, flashing his perfect white teeth.

I know what my words mean, to both the guard and Juliet. They assume Percival was sneaking into the house for a late night tryst with me. It's better than telling them the truth, so I have to let it go. Juliet's concerned look remains, but it changes slightly. Now there's a suspicious quality to it, which makes sense. She's only rarely laid eyes on Percival, and never in such close quarters or so late at night. She's been my friend and worked for the family for many years, and her natural, almost maternal, instincts to protect me kick into gear. I love her more for it. Though in a way, it makes me sad. It should be my mother, or my father, coming out of that elevator. Not Juliet.

The guard asks if he has my permission to look around, make sure nothing else unusual is going on, and I nod. I know what he'll find — the terrace door open, or at least unlocked. That's sure to cement the idea that Percival and I are having a secret rendezvous. Whatever. He'll wonder how Percival possibly got up there, but here's the deal: my family *pays* for this security. He's not a cop. I don't have to answer any questions, and I don't even have to make sense. If I say a friend came in, and he happened to come in from the roof, then that's what happened. Thanks for your dutiful service, no need to dig any further. Every once in a while, Kevin's money — fine, *our* money — comes in handy.

After the security officer is done, he nods and wishes us a good night, though I catch a tiny uptick at the corners of his mouth. *My night's not going to be anything like what you're imagining, buddy*, I think. The two reenter the elevator, leaving Percival and me alone once more.

Percival suddenly sucks in a sharp breath. "We need to call Zee — she could be in danger."

He's right, of course. If one of us was targeted, why not the others? We were EM outlaws now, and we had to band together. I quickly tapped Zee on speed dial.

One ring, two. *Come on.* A third ring...

"Jesus, Lyn, I'm *sleeping*," Zee says groggily.

"Well, I'm not, and neither is Percival," I reply, and just like the guard, I think Zee jumps to the wrong conclusion.

"So glad you called to inform me of that. Good night." I hear her fumble with her phone.

"Wait! Zee! This is important — it's not what you think. Percival came to my house because he was attacked. By a Stickman. You could be next. I want you to come over here, so we can all be together."

"A Stickman?" she asks, slowly sounding more awake. "Where?"

"His house," I say.

Zee gasps. "They tracked him... home? How?"

"No idea, but if they tracked him..."

"You can stop there," Zee says. "I'm getting dressed and will see you shortly. I'll grab a cab."

"Don't bother," I say. "I'll have a car waiting for you. Move fast, and be careful." I cut the line without waiting for her to reply, tap another speed dial option, and in moments Kevin's car service is heading for Zee's building. We have the unlimited service option, so I know that this little special trip won't result in some invoice or bill that my brother will quiz me about. I know. I know. Tough life. Well, at least that part isn't tough.

———

I TEXT Juliet to tell her Mackenzie's coming over, and I can feel her confusion when she replies.

Okay...

If she thinks Percival has come over with romantic intentions, she must be really confused why Zee is joining us. I don't want her thinking something really kinky is about to happen, so I tell her enough of the truth to change her mind.

Our friend died. We need to commiserate together. Sorry it's so late at night.

I can almost hear the relief in her response. *Of course. Completely understand. I'll send her up when she arrives.*

Thanks, J! I send back, followed by a little red heart. She's the best.

———

BELIEVE IT OR NOT, I think you can count the number of times my very best friend Mackenzie has been inside my house on one hand, or if not, you wouldn't need more than just your ten fingers. I'm ashamed of both aspects — my over-the-top home life and privilege, and how keeping her away feels like shunning my friend. But it's time to move on from those feelings. We need to be together, all of us.

"Your room... hasn't changed," Zee says with a wry smile.

"Shut up," I reply.

She pauses in her examination of my room long enough to ask the question on everyone's mind. "Do you think one will come for us? Tonight?"

I shrug. "No idea. But there's something important Percival needs to tell you."

Zee tilts her head, suspicious. "What?"

For his part, Percival looks like he would rather jump out the window, even if there was a Stickman waiting below, than tell Mackenzie what he's about to say. "Zee, look, I guess I can't be sure, but I think, um..." He squirms and fiddles with his blond locks.

"Say it," Zee says, in a way that tells me she's already guessed. "Say it."

"I think the Stickman that attacked me might have been Robin," he says, all in a hurry to get it out.

Her knees buckle and Zee drops down to sit on my bed, her entire body drooping like she's losing air. In a way, it looks like she can't breathe, so I guess she really is losing air. My heart thumps loudly in my chest, feeling like its pushing at my ribs, even my throat. I want to cry, or scream, or kill whoever's responsible. But who's responsible for a Stickman? No one. They just *are*.

"And if he comes here...?" she finally says.

It was the obvious next thought, and I wanted to word my response delicately. I swiped away tears and sat next to my friend, putting an arm over her shoulders, letting her lean into me. "If he does, we help him by stopping him. We give him peace."

"And if we fail?" Zee asks.

Percival looks up, having just been through that very scenario. "We run."

21

NOWHERE IS SAFE

Two floors below, Juliet screams.

I sit up in shock, followed by Zee on the other side of the bed. Percival jumps up off the floor. We had been talking in that configuration, not intending to sleep, but sleep is sort of like that. Amazing how we have our natural youthful energies plus deep wells of EM power, but we can't manage to stay up one entire night without zonking. Sort of pathetic actually. And now Juliet is in trouble.

"Come on," I say, flying through the door, not waiting for a response. I take the stairs down several steps at a time, in a way I haven't done since I was a kid, even jumping down to the landing. I'm keenly aware of the contrast with those happier days. The general commotion I hear above tells me Zee and Percival are following, which is good because I'm pretty sure I know what I'll find when I reach the main floor, and I'd rather not be solo when that happens.

"Juliet!" I shout, taking the next flight down. "We're coming!"

Just below me, I hear Juliet, not responding to me, but at least alive. At least talking. "What in God's name *are* you?"

I jump down to the floor of the entryway, nearly knocking over Juliet, and I'm immediately in a pickle. In the open door that leads toward the back of the house is a Stickman. And damn if it doesn't resemble Robin. If a burned out husk of a human being with blackened eyes and charred skin can resemble anyone, truly. *Why him?* I think. But there's not time for anything but defense, and that means using my electromagic. In front of Juliet.

"Sorry about this," I say to her as I call up my energy. The Stickman — Robin — dives forward, toward me, and I have the presence to shove Juliet behind me and into the front room of the house. I know my body is glowing faintly blue in the dim light, and I probably just gave her a little inadvertent shock, but I'll just have to figure out what to say to Juliet afterward. If I live that long.

I fire a bolt of electromagic directly into the belly of the charging Stickman, but it's wickedly fast. It dodges left and seems to leap off the wall, still coming at me. I take aim a second time and fire, missing again. The room is too small. The Stickman is too close. I have a millisecond to think about what it might be like to join Robin. Will he recognize me? Do Stickmen really communicate? Or will I just be lost, forever?

I cringe back, firing upward, certain I'll miss again and the Stickman will fall on me. And then, you know what it'll be... *A-th-th-the That's all, folks! Good morning, good afternoon, and good night, New York City!* I am a goner.

Two bolts of energy blast over my head, pummeling the Stickman into the wall, and knocking it away from me. I sheepishly look up to see Zee and Percival at the bend of the stairs, both glowing with power. I'm keenly aware of how this all must look to Juliet, but there's nothing I can do about it unless I want to turn and explain the situation to her. That doesn't seem wise with a Stickman still in the room.

"Sure took your sweet time getting here," I mutter as I stand up.

"If you ask me, we got here just at the right time," Zee says, dripping with snark. They step down into the vestibule and now it's three on one. We all raise our hands to fire at the Stickman — at our friend, Robin — instinctively arraying ourselves to cover the left, middle, and right portions of the room. Anywhere he goes, we'll get him.

But Robin the Stickman turns and flees down the hall toward the back of the house, quickly lost in darkness. I guess even Stickmen have some sense of awareness and a desire for self-preservation. Crap.

For a moment, all of us just stare. Then I remember Juliet is behind me and just witnessed all three of us shooting electricity out of our fingertips. That had to be weird. I turn. "Juliet, um, let me explain..."

She replies like she isn't interested in what I have to say. "The back stairs," she says in a hushed tone.

"Ah crap," I say. She's right. We have two stairways in the town-house — the front one we just came down, and a back one.

"What?" Percival says. "What about the back stairs."

"There's another staircase in the back of the house," I say. I point a finger in the direction the Stickman went, then loop it up and back toward us. "If that Stickman goes up, it can circle back and come right down the front stairs." Suddenly we all find it necessary to edge away from the steps. "Or it could hide, anywhere really. We need to make sure it's gone."

"Come on then," Percival says, heading toward the back of the house.

I grab his arm to stop him. "Hold on, I'll go that way. I know the house. You two, go up the front stairs. We'll surround it. Er, him." I glance sideways at Zee, hoping that calling the Stickman Robin an "it" didn't offend her.

"*It*," she says, like a declaration. "That's not Robin anymore. And if we can destroy it, we destroy it. Come on." With a determined step, Zee leads Percival up the front stairs. "We release what used to be Robin into peace."

I turn back to Juliet, and my tone is half apology, half pleading. "I'll have to explain later. Please stay here." Wide-eyed, she nods, and that has to do for now. I run into the dark hallway toward the back of the house.

———

IT'S STRANGE. The back section of the first floor is not a place I've often visited; it's Juliet's realm. To one side is the door to her room, and the second door is what we call Juliet's bathroom. In the decades I've lived in the house, I might have used that bathroom a dozen times, mostly when I was a young kid who couldn't wait to pee upstairs. The staircase is on my right, opposite those doors, but I have to check one thing first. The kitchen sits open at the back of the house, and beyond that is a small outdoor garden. Flicking on the kitchen light, the force of my pampered, privileged life hits me like a tsunami. *When was the last time I set foot in this room?* Still, there's no time for self-examination and recrimination. I scan the room, but there's no sign of a Stickman.

Sure enough, the door to the garden is open — that must be how it got in. And hopefully, that's how it got out. Quickly, I shut the door, lock it, then turn on the outside light. The garden is empty. *Good riddance*, I think. I have maybe two seconds of relief before I hear something knocked over upstairs. *Shit. It did take the back stairs.* I have a vision of the Stickman attacking my friends, and that spurs me to action.

Back into the hallway, I hit the stairs in a sprint. There's a yellow-white glow coming from above, which means Zee and Percival are there. I doubt the Stickman bothers to turn on the overhead lights. When I reach the top, I quickly look left and right, wary of attack from any side. Thankfully, the layout on the second floor is open enough that I can see all the way to the front and back of the house. The dining room on my right looks empty. To my left, the living room and library also appear devoid of life. *Upstairs!* I think, rounding back into the next flight.

But I know the third floor is quite a bit different. It's not open. The back stairs only go to the back bedroom, and there's no way to get to the front rooms — like my bedroom — from there, unless...

I hear a window shatter just above.

Unless the thing goes out the window.

I'm sure Percival and Zee heard the noise, too, so I hurry to the top of the stairs. There, the window directly in front of me has been blasted outward, but there's no sign of the Stickman in the space outside. Leaning my head out, I see the windows to my own bedroom on my left. One of those is shattered, too.

And standing next to my bed with its back turned to me is Robin, the Stickman.

Well, isn't this a little freaking surreal? I think. But I'm offended. The thing is in *my* room. I slink through the first broken window, avoiding any shards that might cut me, and step gingerly toward the second. It still has its back to me as I slip into my own room in a way I never dreamed I'd do. Standing inside, I realize what a stupid move I just made. I'm now in a small room with a Stickman. That was not well planned.

But it continues to look the other way. Somehow I've managed to sneak up on it. In my life, I've only ever seen a Stickman a few times, and most of those have been in the past few days, always in a frenzy of motion. I've never seen one standing completely still. What the hell is it doing?

The Stickman's body stiffens briefly and I hear a sound of inhaled air. *It's... sniffing? For what?* Then it hits me. *Oh my God. Can they smell us?* The thing must have been drawn to my room like a shark to blood in the water.

Honestly, that freaks me out even more.

A creepy Stickman is in my room, and it's *sniffing* for me. That's my cue to be just about fed up with all this crap, so I pull as much energy as I can inward. I can tell my EM powers are lessening — I'd used an awful lot so far. But I remember what Torden said, about my Quotient. I can make power go farther than others. Time to put that shit to the test.

I fire, with everything I have.

I guess I waited just a tad too long, because the Stickman starts to turn. He's noticed me. He jumps. I jump. Firing again, I roll forward. He dives away. Then I'm near the door and suddenly Zee and Percival are by my side. The Stickman skitters out the open window and we see it standing outside like a shadow in the night.

"Yeah, you better run!" I shout at it, fist raised.

Suddenly two dark figures drop down from above — probably from the roof terrace. They land in a crouch, then rise. In the blue glow of night, the silhouettes of three Stickmen stand before us.

In my life, I've never heard of three Stickmen in the same place at the same time. Immediately my bravado disappears, a candle blown out by a hurricane. "Yeah, we better run," I say, grabbing Zee and Percival each by the arm and pushing them toward the front stairs.

22

HEADLONG FLIGHT

I can't just leave Juliet in a house full of Stickmen, can I? I mean, maybe they won't bother her — she's not an EM, after all. But now she's seen things. That will definitely change my relationship with her. I hope it's not reason enough for the Stickmen to make her a target. No, that's impossible, right? Stickmen don't *think*, do they?

Maybe they do. I mean, they came together, the three of them. Isn't that some sort of advanced animal behavior — pack hunting? Plus, I didn't know they could smell us until about a minute ago, so there's that. I can't exactly call myself an expert on the subject.

They might harm Juliet just because she's in the way. I can't let that happen.

I freeze at the bottom of the stairs and Zee slams into my back. Percival stops a couple centimeters before doing the same.

"Move, Lyn — come on!" Zee says.

I turn my head to look up the stairs and one of the Stickmen appears. *Good*, I think. *Follow me.* I start to move again, passing through the entryway toward the front door. Juliet appears on my right, just what I don't want to see. I hold a palm out, facing her. "Stop! Go back, for your own safety." That's when I notice the phone in her hand. Juliet carefully backs away. I pull open the front door but once again pause.

It's Percival's turn to complain. "Lyn, come on — let's go. They're right behind us."

I meet his eyes and then nod over his shoulder toward Juliet, not just some random employee of the family, but my lifelong friend. "I have to make sure those things follow us. *All* of them."

"Come home safe and sound, you hear me?" Juliet says with raw sincerity, her voice cracking. Whatever's going on with the monster in the house, it's life-threatening. She might not understand everything, but she understands that.

I nod. "Make the call," I say. *No one will believe what happened here tonight anyway.*

She starts to dial a number, short and fast. 9-1-1.

"Lyn, we do this together," Percival says with a confidence that I grab onto like a life vest. Over the years, Percival has worn the mantle of being beautiful but stupid pretty well. But I know it isn't the full truth. Sure, he's beautiful, but he's smarter than most people think. He immediately understands me, tossing back a wave of curly blond hair before moving to one side, ready. Zee slides to my other side.

And then it appears. The first Stickman. The one that looks like Robin, if Robin was an overcooked Thanksgiving turkey. From such a close distance, I can see the singed curls of flesh that appear ready to flake off him at any moment. It's repulsive. Still, I wait. And for some reason, so does the Stickman.

But we don't have to wait long, as the other two crowd the stairwell behind just moments later. *Okay*, I think. *Just follow us outside.* I reach behind and pull open the front door. "Now! Go!" I shout, stirring Percival and Zee to bolt through the doorway and into the night. I start to back out, keeping an eye on the Stickmen.

The one in front, Robin, turns its charred head toward Juliet, who's still retreating toward the back of the house. "Hey! You want a charge, you gotta come this way!" That gets its attention. Maybe too well. Suddenly the three Stickmen are pushing at each other trying to get to me, so I step backward into the small front garden that separates our house from the street. Zee grabs me by the shirt and pulls me through the front gate, then we're running down the sidewalk. A quick glance behind shows that all three Stickmen have followed us out.

Phew, okay, Juliet's safe, I think, before realizing that I have to figure out what to do about being chased through New York City by a trio of monsters. Now what?

Thankfully, Percival decides to take charge, at least for a moment. "This way," he says, ducking into an alley on our left.

We run, headlong to who knows where.

There's nothing particularly remarkable about an EM's ability to do normal human things, and I'm no track star, so not surprisingly, the Stickmen gain on us. Fear and adrenaline stoke me to run faster, but it's pretty unlikely any of us are going to win this footrace. Even Percival, who's the tallest and most athletic, isn't going to stay ahead of the Stickmen and their frenetic pace for long.

"We need to do something else," Zee says between panting breaths.

I get an idea. "Keep heading toward the park." Percival zigs right on Lexington, and we follow. There are people all around, because this is the city that never sleeps, of course. For us, though, that's a bad thing. We can't really use our power, not out in the open. Not yet. Still it helps, because the Stickmen seem to inherently avoid people, too, and rather than follow us down the sideway, they disappear behind a building. I slow my pace, as does Zee. Percival relaxes and turns back, but something catches his eye behind us. He's looking upward. Somehow I know what he's seeing without looking, but I follow his eyes anyway. The Stickmen are skittering over rooftops, still coming for us. I suck in a deep breath. "Well, crap. That's not good. Go!" Pushing Percival forward, I leap into a renewed sprint.

"If we stay on the ground," Zee asks, panting hard, "won't they avoid us? There are people around." Thankfully, she doesn't slow down while talking.

"No good," I say. "They came into my house with Juliet there. We can't bet our lives on a Stickman being afraid to appear in public."

"Let's cross here," Percival says. "If those things want to climb buildings, we can put a little pavement between us." As he passes a large, Gothic-looking cathedral — I should know the name of it, this close to my house, but I don't, sorry — he cuts left to head down East 66th. I only know the street names because their written on the signs we pass.

It's a bad idea, but nonetheless I crane my neck around to see where the Stickmen are. There, high atop the cathedral, I see them, all three. They look like gargoyles on the edges of the roofline, and if I didn't know any better, I believe that's what they really are. *Ha, you bastards. See you later*, I think, as the wide gap of Lexington Avenue leaves them far behind us. I'm about to face forward again, and I'm even thinking of telling the others to slow down, when I see something unbelievable and terrifying. One of the Stickmen hunkers down and then leaps across the intersection diagonally, coming to rest on top of the big red armory building to our right. As the other two Stickmen tense to follow, I whip my head around. "You guys, they just jumped across the street." My fear gives me another burst of speed and I pass Percival.

"They can do that?" he asks, incredulous.

"Apparently so," I say, pointing toward the top of the armory where the first Stickman is mirroring our run at street level.

"Shit," Zee says, and I agree.

Seconds later, all three Stickmen are scrambling just above us. I lead us to the other side of East 65th, just to avoid having a Stickman drop on my head unexpectedly. We hit Park Avenue and race out into the intersection against the light. Cabs honk, but that's not exactly an odd thing in the city. Sure, we're the only people running, but we're definitely not the only strange sight people will see in New York on this night, so we keep moving and hope that we're forgotten as soon as we pass. Central Park is now two long blocks in front of us, and everyone buckles down to run those blocks as fast as we possibly can.

"You thinking what I'm thinking?" Percival asks.

"You know it," I say. "Zee?"

"I'll beat you there," she replies, arms pumping as she gains a step or two on us.

Still, two blocks going west seems like an impossible distance. "Why did they make these blocks so *long* in this direction?" No one answers. What good would an answer do anyway? We've all lived here long enough to know that crossing two more avenues means about a half mile. I think my heart is going to burst.

Above, the Stickmen do their crazy leap thing to get them on the same side of the street we're on, and that's enough to make me stop caring about an elevated pulse and start worrying about having all the power sucked out of me by a monstrous electric sponge. We cross Madison to the tune of many more blaring horns. *Quarter mile or so, then the park. Come on.*

"Oh no," Zee says, pointing forward.

She doesn't need to explain. Construction is ubiquitous in the city, and on any normal occasion, I wouldn't give the scaffolding shielding the sidewalk on both sides of the street a second thought. It's as common as breathing to walk through the structures, though you have to be careful not to get surprised in there by creeps or muggers. This is not a normal occasion. The creeps we're concerned about would be dropping down onto that scaffolding from above. They could attack us from close range and we wouldn't be likely to see them coming.

"Run faster, please," Percival says, nodding toward the park just ahead. I'm wondering which covered walkway he'll choose, when suddenly Percival picks Option C — the middle of the road, into oncoming traffic.

A small truck screeches to a halt, just missing him. The driver offers us some free advice on where to walk in the city, as well as what we could do with ourselves in the meantime. I wave the single-finger salute, thanking him for his kind words. Dodging other vehicles, I see something dark hit the top of the scaffolding on my left. "Guys — Coming in from the left side!" In response, Percival guides us around a cab toward the other side of the street, but that's suddenly a bad idea, too. A second Stickman drops down to the covered walkway on that side, and we're hemmed in. I'm wondering where the third Stickman is when it decides to reveal itself, leaping onto a streetlight just to our left. I don't think. I know the ramifications of using my power in front of normal people, but I have to do something. The only other choice is being surrounded and killed by Stickmen.

Running just underneath the streetlight, I quickly pull in my electromagic and send a harsh bolt of energy up the pole, directly toward the Stickman. It's not likely to hurt the thing, but it does have the effect I was hoping for, exploding the streetlight in a huge burst of sparks and a blaze of light.

It's just enough. We reach Fifth Avenue and dart across, leaping over the short stone wall that surrounds this part of Central Park. Percival, Zee, and I duck into the dense trees then fill ourselves with power, each of us suddenly glowing blue light. Without a word, we lift ourselves into the sky and zip like strange human sparks, heading north as fast as possible and staying low over the dark trees to avoid as many eyes as we can.

23

THIEVES IN THE NIGHT

S till breathless, we fly past the large reservoir and land in a dark grassy area littered with baseball diamonds, somewhere in the northern part of Central Park. Nighttime in the city is not like other places. The glow of all those lights mutes the effects of the dark. But here in the middle of the park, the night takes on an ominous feel, especially since we're running for our lives. Central Park is known not to be particularly safe after dark, and we feel it, just not for the same reasons as most other people.

"Well, *hello*," a male voice says with a sort of sinister glee from behind us. No wonder the park gets a bad rap.

"You girls lost?" a second male voice says. Then there's laughter. Sounds like three, total. We all turn around to face our new acquaintances.

Three thugs hanging out in the park at night with no idea who they're messing with.

"Listen, fellas," Percival says with his hands up and palms forward, assumedly a pointless peace offering. "We're on our way out of here. No need for trouble."

"Trouble?" The tallest of the group says with a wrinkled up face, before turning to the one on his left. "Opus? You think there's trouble here?" The trio walks closer, and while I think maybe we should back away, I instinctively know that doing so would show fear, and would just get these three even more motivated to mess with us.

The pale twenty-something with a close crop of curly hair so light it might be white, grins and shakes his head. Assumedly, his name is *Opus*. Who on Earth names a kid Opus? Maybe it's just a crappy nickname. "No trouble here." They keep walking, closing the distance between us.

The middle thug turns to his right. "Chico?" *What's with these guys and their names?* I think.

Chico, shorter and thicker, dark hair, stares at us — particularly me — intently. It makes my skin crawl. I know this type of guy, and being stuck in the dark in the park with such a creep is an intensely unpleasant feeling. "I don't see a problem." He smiles, revealing the gap where a tooth used to be, smack in the middle of his upper row of front teeth. *Is this guy a hockey player or something?* I think, knowing that guys who roam Central Park after dark are unlikely to be hockey players. Though there is a skating rink, so maybe... "What's your name, girl?" he says to me, lecherously.

I cross my arms. "I'm *not* a girl."

Percival is keenly aware of what's happening and steps in front of me, a human shield. While I appreciate the chivalry, I'm still a little offended, though, I have to admit, less offended than I have been in the past. "That's enough," Percival says.

The short one, Chico, looks at his taller companion, assumedly the boss of this little joke of a gang. "Heh. Is that enough, Johnny?"

Johnny's smile drops. Now he's serious. "Nope. We're just getting started." Finally, they stop within arms' reach of us, conveniently arrayed so that each one of them covers one of us, no doubt assuming that Percival can't defend us all this way.

Suddenly there's static in my head. "Short blast?" Percival says, using our special way of talking that the three dopes in front of us can't hear.

"Yep," Zee replies. She sounds positively giddy.

"Indubitably," I add, a smile dawning across my face.

The short one, Chico, notices. "Hey look, Johnny. She looks like she's happy to see us."

"Why shouldn't she be?" Johnny replies. "We'll show her and her friend a real good time." He looks from me to Zee and back, skimming past Percival like he's not even there. They start to laugh, all three of them.

Percival's voice comes through on the static airwaves again. "Just a quick jolt, then stop. One." That's all he says, but his meaning is clear.

"Two," Zee says, her tone now brimming with anticipation.

I wait a moment, letting the thugs laugh before adding my own, final number to the count, saying it out loud because I really want to see the look of confusion on their faces before it all happens. "Three."

The gang of fools before us has a moment to look even more stupid than usual before Percival, Zee, and I each lash out with a controlled burst of electromagic.

We do our best to keep the blast simple and short, but it's not called *electroscience* for a reason. If we go too far, well, we didn't pick the fight, did we?

Writhing from the electric shocks, the three thugs drop to the ground in convulsions, faint arcs of blue lightning tracing up and down their bodies before finally everything goes still and dark.

Percival leans down and checks on them, one at a time.

"Out cold?" Zee asks, sounding somewhat nervous, somewhat hopeful. It isn't often we use our powers on normal people, so we don't have a completely firm grasp on how much it might take to kill them.

Percival stands and nods. I remember vaguely that he's a guy who gets paid to do odd jobs he doesn't want to talk about. Maybe one of us really does have experience zapping people till they pass out. "Let's head north out of the park and get the hell out of here. I don't want to go back south and risk bumping into those Stickmen."

"Good idea," I say, as Zee and I follow his lead.

———

WALKING through trees in near-complete darkness, at least for New York, my mind begins to wander. *What's going on? Stickmen. Torden. The High Order. Am I just completely out of touch, or has something changed?*

We're almost out of the park when we sense rather than see that someone is following us. "These guys don't know when to quit," Zee says, as we all turn around. "Hey—!" she yells before Percival clamps his hand over her mouth.

I almost object, but I can see from Percival's eyes that something is wrong. Zee offers a muffled complaint, but she, too, sees he's serious. Percival looks back toward the south, and suddenly all is clear.

In the distance, a Stickman is walking toward us through the woods, only appearing intermittently in bands of light as it steps between the trees. It moves surprisingly slowly, with a surprising sense of purpose.

"Jesus, again?" I whisper harshly.

Percival gives me a stern look before speaking via our static channel. "Can you be quiet? I don't think it sees us yet — see? It's just walking. Come on." He releases Zee and guides us to one side, out of the path of the approaching Stickman by a good distance. We duck behind a huge oak.

"What if it, you know, smells us or something?" Zee says, popping in my mental ears.

"We fly again," Percival replies.

We wait. It approaches. We're off to one side of its path a good distance, hoping that we're far enough away that it can't smell us. And then, as it passes... it just keeps going, heading north. In a few minutes, we start to lose sight of it among the dense trees.

Percival steps out from behind the tree and starts to follow it, heading north. "Let's go," he says. "Close enough to see it, not close enough for it to sense us."

"Why?" I ask.

He turns and gives me a serious look. "We need to figure out where its going. More importantly, we need to figure out what the hell is going on around here."

24

THE WRITHING IN THE PIT

I t takes most of the night, but we keep after the Stickman, following it at a distance. Outside of Central Park, things get weird. Stickmen like to skitter up walls and use rooftops when traveling in town, just as we saw when they chased us. I guess walking down the street for something as clearly monstrous and inhuman as a Stickman is a bad idea. We keep to street level, each of us far enough apart to triangulate its movements, slowly creeping north and east through town.

When it reaches the Harlem River, it picks up some friends. Three, to be exact. Invariably the three that chased us out of my house.

Zee catches my eye from down the block, holding up four fingers. "What the hell is going on around here?" she says via our static connection. Since I have no idea, I don't bother to reply. *My thoughts exactly.*

As if we needed more proof that Stickmen were bizarro freaks of nature — assuming nature is truly responsible for them — the four climb *underneath* one of the bridges crossing the river.

"Are they crossing, or just hiding?" Zee says, as we reconvene a short ways from the bridge.

"Crossing, I think," I say.

"One way to find out," Percival says, striding forward to cross.

"What if they *live* under there?" Zee says. "Like the troll in the fairy tale?"

"Then I guess we're the three billy goats," Percival says, still walking.

I scoff and rush to catch up. "You're very casual for someone who might get turned into a Stickman in the next 30 seconds."

He smiles. "Doesn't seem to be stopping you, either. How come? Would you miss me?"

I punch his arm. Zee jogs to join us as we start to cross. Thankfully there's a pedestrian walkway on one side, separated from four lanes of traffic by a low wall. By New York standards, there aren't a lot of cars crossing the bridge, but then again it is the middle of the night. Still, the ones that do cross blind us with their headlights as they pass. I find myself hoping that momentary blindness doesn't result in us stumbling into a flock of Stickmen, but then the lights actually do us a favor. As a pair of cars go by, their lights illuminate something moving near the other side of the bridge. Four somethings, dark and running away from us. I kinda wonder if the driver notices, but I suppose in the dark, with only a fleeting glimpse, a Stickman might pass for a human being, especially since at one point said Stickmen actually *were* human beings. Of course, even if a normal person saw a Stickman plain as day, my guess is that their mind would try to rationalize it. Maybe it's a burn victim, or a costume. Because it can't be a living, walking electromagic sponge creature, right? Right.

Once we're across the bridge and into the Bronx, we repeat the process of triangulation to track the Stickmen, though with four of them it's a notably more nerve-racking affair. Two or three times, the Stickmen stop, and we fear we've been noticed, but our luck holds. Their northeast track remains pretty true, like they're either a weird sort of migratory bird, or following a homing beacon, or... who knows? Maybe they share a condo near the zoo.

"You guys, this is bad," Zee says in our static connection.

"Four Stickmen together?" I say. "Of course it's bad."

"No, not just that," she replies. "Aren't you worried where they're going?"

I stop. Something about it felt bad from the beginning. Four Stickmen following a path to somewhere like they were homing pigeons. "Being drawn to some place..." I say aloud.

"What?" Percival asks, looking back over his shoulder while still trying to track the Stickmen from afar.

"They're going to the pavilion." There. I said it. Spitting out the idea that had been slowly forming in my head is as liberating as it is terrifying.

"To do what?" Percival asks. "Attack? Then we need to get there first — to warn them."

"If they'll even listen to us," Zee says, and suddenly we all see the dilemma of our situation.

But I'm not sure. "What if...?"

"Spit it out, Lyn," Zee says.

"What if they aren't going there to attack, they're going there because that's their home?" I pause to let that set in. For myself, too. Because that's a crazy idea. A song pops into my head, taking on an ominous tone. *I'm on my way, I'm on my waaaaaay, home sweet home.*

Percival rounds to face me. "Are you trying to tell me that Torden keeps Stickmen like pets? How? They try to *kill us* on sight, and there are EMs all over that place. Even if he wanted to, how would it not become a bloodbath?"

"I have no idea, but we'd better go find out." I push past Percival, seeing the Stickmen skitter up a building and out of view. I need to hurry, to catch up.

———

IT'S NEARLY impossible to track the Stickmen once we get to the park that surrounds Torden's pavilion, but there isn't much need. By that time, it's pretty obvious where we're all going.

"We should zip ahead," I tell the others, static popping. They nod, and a second later we're in flight. Yes, we emit that faint blue glow, but in the darkness of the trees, it's doubtful anyone sees us. Moments later, we're on the south section of the beach, near where we mourned Robin not so long ago, and knowing he's one of the Stickmen coming toward us. We turn to look at the buildings behind us, silent and motionless, waiting for the Stickmen to show themselves. And they do. Up on the roof of the south wing. The coincidence is not lost on any of us.

We found a captive Stickman there. And now, four other Stickmen are lowering themselves into something atop the building, disappearing from our view one by one.

"We've gotta get up there," Percival says.

"Come on, Pers, that's suicide," Zee replies. "If we get too close, and they jump us..." There wasn't a need to elaborate. Robin's charred face was still an image staining my vision.

"She's right," I say, and Zee nods, thinking I've seen the sense in her concern. And I have, but, you know, I'm not always one to *act* sensibly, even if I see the sensible way. "But we have to go anyway."

"What?" Zee says, shocked.

"Look at it like this, Zee. If we don't go, we don't really know if Torden and the others are at risk, living right next to a pod of Stickmen they might not even know about, or if there's something else going on here. If we don't go and check it out, how can we know who to trust?"

Zee shakes her head. "There's got to be another way. I— I'm terrified of those things. Following them at a distance was one thing. Sticking my head into their bedroom is quite another."

"Then I'll do it. You guys wait here," I say.

"No, I should go," Percival says.

"What have I told you about this sexist bullshit, Pers?" I cross my arms.

"Fine," he says. "*We* can both go. Zee, you can stay here."

"And live in shame forever," she replies. "No, you know we're all going. But I'll tell you this — if I die, I am *not* going to forgive you. Neither one of you."

"Um... deal. I guess," I say. Then I pull in my electromagic power and start to glow, dashing upward toward the rooftop. Percival launches himself after me.

"Jesus," Zee says, static in my head.

I pause and turn back, hovering in midair. "What's wrong?"

"I just didn't know we were going so fast, I guess," she replies, still standing on the beach.

"Would you rather we crept in all spy-like?" Percival chides.

Zee grunts her disapproval before floating up to meet us. "Definitely not. Let's go." Oddly enough, she leads the way. Over the roof, she lowers herself gently until her feet touch down without a sound. She douses her power. We follow her lead, soon standing as a trio on the roof of the south wing.

"See that?" Percival says, pointing toward the middle of the roof. "There's a skylight or something. A way in."

Zee visibly shakes, her nerves taking over her body physically. "You guys, what is it we've been told from Day One? *If you see a Stickman, you run.* And yet, we followed one across town. Stupid. And then that one gathered some friends and we followed all four of them even farther. *Really* stupid. Now we want to stick our heads into that opening, where we *know* they went? Unbelievably stupid. We must all have a death wish."

"Zee—" I start.

She turns to me with tears in her eyes. "I don't want to die, Lyn. I don't want it to happen, what they did to Robin. I can't."

I lean in and give her a hug. Whispering in her ear, I try to settle her down. "Just stay here a second. I won't go inside. I'll just look. Okay?" At first she doesn't answer. "Okay?" I repeat. Head next to mine, I feel her nod. Gently I push away and turn toward the skylight, or whatever it is. I creep slowly forward, noticing that even Percival isn't walking with me. *Guess he's putting that chivalry crap on pause. Good.*

At the side of the hole, I stop, then carefully and oh so slowly lean my head over the edge. It's dark, so dark I can't make out a thing. My body almost starts to shiver in fear, mimicking Mackenzie, but I will it to stop. I will my eyes to adjust, to see whatever there is, down in the dark.

Then it happens.

"Oh my God," I breath, barely audible.

"What?" Zee asks using our static connection. "What is it, Lyn?"

I back up, almost stumbling, just wanting — no *needing* — to get away from this place. Not looking, I run directly into Percival, who grabs my arms to steady me. "What did you see?"

"It— it's like a pit full of them. Dozens, maybe hundreds."

"Stickmen?" Zee says with new terror in her voice. And here we thought a group of four was unbelievable. "Hundreds?"

I lock eyes with her. "That isn't the worst of it."

Zee stares. "Hundreds of Stickmen *isn't* the worst of it. Oh good-ie." She looks like she might faint.

Suddenly we all realize exactly the danger we're in. Maybe we could fend off one. If we were the luckiest bastards on earth, we could manage the four. But hundreds? If we startled them out of their pit and they overwhelmed us before we could escape, we were very, very dead. No worse. We'd be like them. Stickmen forevermore, doomed to live in that pit.

And still, there was that other thing. "There's something bigger down there," I say. "I couldn't see it clearly enough, but it made the Stickmen look tiny in comparison."

Percival looks like his blood has turned to ice. "Hundreds of Stickmen *and* something much bigger. Right. Well, this has been a full night, hasn't it?" He dons a smile that quickly evaporates in the current mood. "But... do they know? Does Torden know, or is he sitting on top of a hornet's nest? Or a lion's den?" Percival asks. "Or I don't know what. A giant's lair?"

Off the side of the building next to us, we hear a voice, and we all jump. A moment later we realize Stickmen don't talk. But is that a good thing or a bad thing? We edge to the side of the building and peer over, six eyes in the night looking down.

There, below us, we see two people — two of Torden's clan of

EMs. We can't make out what they're saying but it doesn't matter. After a moment, one leaves and the other turns to stand in his place.

"Changing of the guard," Percival says breathlessly.

I nod. "So he knows. They all do."

Zee looks frantic. "We have to leave. *Now*."

I don't even bother responding, because leaving is the only sensible thing to do after what I've seen. I lead us to the opposite edge of the rooftop, using the building to block any possibility the guard below will see our departure, then we glow with power and dash off to the southwest, putting as much distance as we can between us and Torden's pit of writhing Stickmen monsters, including a massive new thing that has no name.

PART III

WAR OR PEACE

25

FUGITIVES

Not knowing where else to go, and hoping the Stickmen were done raiding houses for the night, we return to my house.

Juliet, I think. *What am I going to tell Juliet?* My feet drop onto the rooftop terrace with a dull double-thud, followed by Zee and Percival. But there are lights. Flashing lights through the windows at the front of the house. *Cops. Juliet called the cops, so, well... guess I can't go back inside. Not tonight at least.* "This was a bad idea. Private security was already out here, and now it's the police. Zee — can we go to your place instead?" Stickmen had come for me and Percival. Seemed better to go somewhere they hadn't been.

Zee chuckles, nervously. "My place isn't exactly spacious for three."

Percival intervenes. "We don't need spacious. We need a place to take a breath."

"Well, if you don't mind taking those breaths while listening to my neighbor's TV through the walls and maybe the smells of whatever those people cook for dinner each night, sure."

"What do they cook for dinner?" Percival says, and Mackenzie shoots him a strong look. "I mean, the times I've been at your place, I've wondered."

"How the hell should I know?" Zee says. "Exotically spiced rancid meats? It smells oddly like a weirdo chicken soup in the hallways, all day, every day. You'd think the others in my building had no jobs and simply prepped dinner 24-7."

"Well," I say, eyeing back and forth between them. "This has been informational. Can we go now?"

"Yeah, we can," Zee says. "But you need to understand something, Lyn. Pers and I are expected at work in the morning."

"Technically, I'm contracted to do several jobs tomorrow. No one's waiting for me at a desk," Percival says.

"Whatever, same thing," Zee replies. "We have commitments."

That thought never once crossed my mind.

I know, I know.

Rich girl problems.

———

AT ZEE'S PLACE, we each feel like we've either dropped a ten thousand pound load off of our backs, or perhaps just gained one. Either way, we all collapse in various corners like it's the end of our energy.

"What was it that you saw, Lyn?" Percival says, flopped on the couch, head lolling. I don't bother correcting him about my name, because frankly I'm not feeling much like *Lightning* at the moment, and I'm too damn tired to argue semantics.

"Something big," I say.

"Details would be useful," Zee replies, slowly rolling one hand around in a circle.

"I... I really don't know," I say, trying to recall what it was I saw in the pit. The thought of it terrifies me and exhausts me, simultaneously. Trying to make logical sense of it all, I fall asleep.

———

SOMETIMES SLEEP IS A VERY, very bad idea. Like now. I dream. Vividly.

And of course, I dream about *it*. That thing I saw. Only now, it isn't down in some pit full of Stickmen. Now it's loose, and it's after me.

I startle awake so loudly the others do, too. The first pink tints of morning are making the curtains glow like it's opening night for a Broadway musical. And I hate Broadway musicals.

"You okay, Lyn?" Mackenzie is on her bed while I'm on the floor in the living room. In her apartment, this separates us by perhaps a dozen feet. I don't mind that Percival took the couch, not one bit. I like sitting on the floor. Besides, it really ticks off my brother, Kevin, who thinks that in a posh Manhattan townhome, his own sister could at least have the decency to sit on one of the well-appointed chairs once in a while.

"Fine," I say, not sounding fine. In the past five seconds, I've declared disdain for Broadway and mentioned how I like to piss off my brother. Granted, both of those proclamations occurred inside my head, but I am in a decidedly shitty mood.

Zee steps into the doorway. "Uh huh, just like that time at the library with Mar—"

"Mackenzie," I start sharply. "If you'd like me to tell tales of your sordid past in front of *Percival*, I'd be more than happy to oblige." Zee dramatically closes her mouth with a clacking of teeth. Good. No need to make my mood shittier.

"What's the matter with you two?" Percival says, rubbing at his eyes.

"What's the matter?" Zee echoes. "Pretty much everything."

"Well, yeah, but other than that?" He smiles, showing off those glowing white, perfect teeth.

"You can be an idiot, Pers," Zee says, trying to sound tough but unable to stop from returning the smile.

"I don't understand at all," I say. "How can it be that the three of us are so out of touch?"

Percival loses the smile. "Explain."

"We've been fed these stories for years. How rare the Stickmen are, how dangerous, how we should avoid them at all costs. And

Torden has been this sort of father figure, helping and guiding the younger EMs. I mean, sure, I never really liked the guy, but I always figured that was just me." I took a breath, but continued before anyone else could interrupt. "Now, Stickmen are everywhere. Torden seems like a mad dictator, and he keeps the damn things like pets, or worse, even experimenting on them, I guess. And now, there's this *bigger* thing. A Stickman Plus, or something." No one laughs. It isn't funny. It wasn't intended to be funny. Giant creatures that could wipe you out of existence are never funny.

"Not to mention, it seems like he's got the rest of them helping out," Percival says.

"How can that be?" Zee asks, sounding as incredulous as I know I feel. "I mean, if *every* other EM in the city is working with Torden, how is it that only the three of us are out of the loop?"

"It doesn't seem possible," Percival says.

"It isn't true," I say. "I know it. There's no way every EM at Torden's pavilion is in on this. No way they're all keeping Stickmen like they run a zoo."

"Well, it would be nice to think that, but —" Percival starts.

"She's right," Zee interrupts. "They *aren't* all in on it. Robin..."

"Right," I say, standing and putting an arm around my friend in her grief. "*Robin* wasn't in on it. And I don't believe Hayden is, either. In fact, think about the attack on the Fuse Box. Most of those folks hang out at the pavilion. I don't think any of them would be down with keeping Stickmen in a closet. Not the way they all freaked out and ran when that one appeared there."

"Isn't that what you're supposed to do? Freak out and run?" Zee asks, weakly.

"Damn straight," Percival says. "But if we believe that many EMs are *not* part of whatever Torden is doing, then who is?"

"Rand," I say. "That's for sure."

Zee wipes away a tear. "And those others — the six that grabbed us where Torden was doing his experiments in the south wing."

"And those guards. Never saw them before either. Heck, I can't recall seeing anyone from that little room they shoved us in more than once or twice before in my life." Percival ticks at his fingers. "What's that, maybe 20, 22, total?"

"Okay, so then we know two things," I say, deciding these things were true partially because I wanted to believe them, had to believe them. "First, Torden, Rand, and 20 or so others are some sort of shady subgroup of EMs, doing something very, very shady with Stickmen. A little Clan of Assholes, lying to our faces since who knows when. And second, that means every *other* EM — not just the three of us, but every single other one, at the pavilion or wherever — is in very grave danger. Plus, I didn't even mention the giant thing I saw."

"Oh yeah, that," Percival says. Funny how something so big and important can slip your mind for a moment when you realize most of your life has been a lie.

26

THE STORM BEFORE THE CALM BEFORE THE STORM

Nose down in my phone, I search. The others do the same. None of us are scanning the news, or stock reports, or anything else regulars might do. We're searching for bad weather. One thing seems certain — we need as much charge as we can get, ASAP.

"There's a pretty strong chance of storms by the lakes," Percival says. He means the Great Lakes, which means all the way across the state. A five or six hour drive, one way. Better than nothing. Percival puts his phone up to one ear.

"Who are you calling?" Zee asks.

"Hayden," Percival says. "I want to see if he and any of the others want to come along."

To say that was an unusual thing to do is an understatement. The times Zee, Pers, and I have gotten a charge together have been rarities. Now Percival was asking to get a whole gang together? Why?

As if reading my mind, Zee says. "Reinforcements." Percival starts talking to Hayden, and a smile dawns on my face. Smart cookie.

"Okay, before they all get here, spill it," Zee demands.

"Huh?" I reply, looking out the window. Clouds are slowly building in the west, and soon we'll be heading that way.

"We need to know, Lyn. Tell us about the big thing you saw."

I gulp in air faster than I should, showing my nerves. I hate that. But it has to be said. "I think I know what Torden's really doing, experimenting on Stickmen. He's making things."

Zee gasps. "Jesus, total mad scientist routine. *Making* things? You mean that big creature you said you saw — you think he made that?"

I nod.

"Describe it, Lyn," Percival says.

I have to think a minute. I hadn't seen the thing very clearly, so I had to try to call up the image in my mind. "It was dark, I looked down through the skylight, into the building, and... there were so many Stickmen. To one side was a large space, even darker than the rest. So dark, I think I assumed it was an opening into another space. But then it moved." Percival and Zee lean in, hanging on my words. "It had two arms, two legs, a head. Basically human form, but blocky and *much* bigger."

"Like, how big?" Percival asks. "Ten feet tall? Bigger? Twice as big as a person? More?"

I cock my head, trying to virtually measure the image in my mind. "Maybe twice as big. That seems about right."

"Okay, so in the neighborhood of 12 feet tall. And you said *blocky*."

"Yeah. So, you know how Torden likes to use the word *Golem* instead of Stickman?"

"I think he thinks it makes him sound smart," Zee says with a wry grin.

"Well, he's wrong. It makes him sound stupid. A golem is creature from folklore, and it's supposed to be made up completely of inanimate matter — rocks, mud, clay. Stickman is a better term because they look shriveled and burnt. A Stickman literally looks like he's made of sticks — bones, of course — wrapped in charred flesh. Calling one of those things a Golem makes no sense at all."

"So then Torden is evil and bad with names," Percival says, giving me side-eye.

I punch him in the arm. "What I'm getting at, smart ass, is that this new creature *is* more like a golem. It looks like it's been pieced together. But even then, I don't think the word truly works, because I don't think the big thing is made up of *inanimate* matter."

"What is it then?" Zee asks.

"I think he built it out of Stickmen."

"How? Like Frankenstein? All sewn together?" Percival asks.

"Don't know — couldn't see it well enough. But it's arms looked like a bundle of stick arms, all wrapped up together. Legs, too — they looked like many stick legs together."

"A Mega Stickman," Percival says. "Or Mega Golem."

"I'd probably just call it a Walking Horror," I say, shivering.

Zee thinks about it for a second, trying to imagine this creature. Bad news for me: I didn't have to imagine it. "Do I even want to ask about the head?"

"No," I say, taking a long, slow breath. "You don't. Because that's the part that gave me my nightmare. When I closed *my* eyes, I could see *its* eyes. All twelve of them."

———

"Torden wouldn't like it if he knew we were with you. You guys are really on his shit list right now," Hayden says as we pile into our limousine. Yes, I called the car service, and yes, I ordered a limousine. A bus really, not one of those classy, low and long limos you might be picturing. This was more like the party bus a group of ladies would take for a winery-hopping bachelorette party. We needed the space. Kevin could yell at me about the cost later, if Torden's Walking Horror didn't get me first. And I know, that's a crap name. Maybe we should call it a Mega Golem instead. Plus, the limo bus had one of those little electric, retractable walls so we could talk in private.

"And yet you're here," Percival says, smiling that smile and clapping Hayden on the shoulder in thanks. "Should I ask why? For all of you?"

I knock on the retractable wall and the driver lowers it enough for me to tell him we're ready; the bus's engine rumbles into action. I ordered the bus because Hayden brought a number of friends along, people we've known for years, but usually only see at random pop-up Fuse Box events, or an occasional visit to the pavilion. You know, back when we were welcome there. In addition to Hayden, there's Mary Tate (drink mixer extraordinaire from the Fuse Box), and five others: Walter, Zeb, Karen, Uma, and Bobby. Ten of us gearing up for a possible confrontation with Torden and his CA. (I am just going to keep calling them his Clan of Assholes until something better pops into my mind. I doubt anything will, as I can't imagine a more appropriate name.) Five women, five men. I wonder about that for a second. Coincidence? Fate? It isn't like we're all going to pair up or anything. I mean, I doubt Zee's much in the mood, and Zeb and Uma are brother and sister, so yeah. Plus, Mary Tate is openly gay. I need to stop thinking thoughts about fate bringing us together in some kind of weird pairings, because that was some fictional bullshit. Still, I notice Zee's smile and felt the thankfulness radiating off of her. She had worried she would be cast off from EMs for the rest of her life, yet here we were in a bus full of them. That mattered.

Hayden shrugs. "I can't speak for everyone, but for me, I like being part of the group at the pavilion, you know — being included in the EM community, I guess you could call it. But sometimes Torden and Rand are a little too, I don't know, *militaristic*. Is that a word?"

"Yes," I say. "And an appropriate one."

"And the whole business of you all being banned sounds like a lot of crap to me," Uma adds. "They say you stole documents. What documents?"

"I have no idea," Zee says. "I didn't steal anything. Why would I? What am I going to do with Torden's *documents*, anyway? Does he even have documents?"

Several of the others laugh. "Yeah, he does," Mary Tate says.

"Mostly he tries to keep historical records, and he's sort of an amateur scientist. That sort of thing. So, you know, it wasn't *impossible* that you might have stolen some of those documents from him. But we've known you a long time. To us, it just didn't seem very likely."

Zee smiles, again brimming with warmness. "Thanks."

"Scientific documents?" Percival muses. "You mean about experiments he's running and stuff like that?"

"Yep," Mary Tate replies.

"So then he has documents about the experiments he's doing in the south yard. Where he's experimenting on a captive Stickman?" Percival says it matter-of-factly, but it hits several of the others like a sledgehammer.

Hayden is the first to pick his jaw up off the floor. "Say what now?"

27

ASKING FOR TROUBLE

I honestly have no idea how EMs survived before the age of instantly-updated weather maps on cell phones. Using those, we easily find our way into the strongest parts of the cold front crossing western New York, and we don't even have to travel all the way to Rochester to do it. A curving band of angry red slices across the map from northeast to southwest, and we stay in it for hours. The best part is that, once we tell our driver that we're storm chasers — a lie, but only a couple of degrees away from the truth — he happily obliges by using his own phone and weather app to keep us heading toward the largest blobs of red we can find. (Our driver is an older, almost stereotypical Italian guy named Reggie. That's only really remarkable because I've known a lot of stereotypical Italian guys, and a number of Reggies, and the two had been mutually exclusive until now.) The worst part, of course, is trying to run off and be struck by lightning without our regular-human driver noticing. Luckily, Hayden had foresight. He asked the others to bring anything that might look vaguely like a scientific instrument, and any long, thin metal object they could find. If Reggie scrutinized our "storm chaser gear" for 30 solid seconds, he'd have seen we had pieces of rusting rebar from the pavilion mixed with oddball electronics like a Geiger counter (no idea why anyone had that), a busted old CB radio, a laser-guided level, and someone's scientific calculator. Oh, and we had wire and black tape, too, supposedly to hook all the crap together. It was a joke, but (a) my family's car service is professional and they're used to looking the other way when the rich people did whatever it was that they did, and (b) we weren't stupid enough to pretend to use any of this stuff in front of Reggie. It was always, "Hey park at the bottom of this wooden hillside, and we'll run up to the top and collect some data," or "Stop here and we'll go behind this building." In the driving rain, not many people are out there likely to see a thing you're doing.

The good news is that everyone brought a heavy raincoat, so at least we could somehow hold up the idea that we weren't lunatics trying to get struck by lightning. Which is exactly what we were.

Anyway, with Reggie's diligent help finding hotspots, we got hit a lot — all of us. I think I've been struck almost twenty times. When you climb a fire escape holding a length of rebar, in the middle of a massive, dark thundercloud, these things happen.

Standing in the rain, I feel someone come up next to me. It's Walter, the oldest of our group. "Excuse me, Lyn."

"Hey," I say, sliding away out of habit. We didn't even need to speak about it as a group — EMs tend to avoid each other when lightning is around. My experience with Percival — getting a charge while we were physically connected — was unique for me, and fairly rare for EMs in general. So it's weird that Walter would come up to me in the storm.

"I knew about the Stickman — the one Torden experiments on," he says. "That doesn't make it right or just, but I wanted you to know that some of us at the pavilion do know. Torden says it's to help us find out more about our enemy, and I guess we all believe that. Or we did." I don't reply, hanging my head in the rain. "Anyway, I just wanted to say that I'm sorry. About your parents," Walter says.

The unexpected subject hits me like a brick to the head. "What?" I say, blinking and shaking my head. "Did you know my mother?" She was an EM. Walter was older. It was possible.

"I knew them both, but not well. Back in the day, some of us would get together. Me, a few of the others, your parents. Even Torden and Rand. But one day, your mom and dad just disappeared, and when EMs disappear without a trace, everyone knows what that means. I can't imagine how hard it must have been — must be — for you."

"You knew both of my parents?" I ask, dumbfounded. My dad was a regular.

Walter laughs nervously. "Of course. I'm quite a bit older than you. All EMs of a certain age hung out back then. Both of your parents were around, a lot."

Both? EMs? My mind reels. *My father was an EM? That's impossible — why didn't he ever tell me?* Nonetheless, the coincidences and oddities suddenly make sense. EMs didn't marry regulars, at least not as far as I could tell. Hiding power from someone that close to you becomes nearly impossible over time. Stupidly, I believed my mother had somehow overcome that, figured out a way to live with my father without him knowing. I actually *admired* that about her.

More importantly, I suddenly realize with a deep sense of guilt that I had, in a way, *blamed* my mother for my father's death. She was an EM — when EMs disappear, as Walter pointed out, the assumption is that a Stickman got them. I always figured that had happened to my mom, and my dad paid the price for being in the wrong place at the wrong time with the wrong person. But if he was an EM, too? She wasn't to blame, and the fact that they both disappeared made more sense. I could forgive her, finally, over a grudge I barely realized I was keeping. But, now, finally learning the truth, could I forgive my father for his silence? Did it really make things any better to think of *both* of my parents as charred, awful Stickmen monsters? No, it didn't. So I stood there, silent, realizing that one parent wasn't as guilty as I thought, while the other wasn't as innocent. A zero sum game.

"Anyway," Walter says, and I startle. Wallowing in my thoughts, I almost forgot he was there. "I just wanted to tell you that. That I'm sorry." He turns and heads down the wooded hillside, back toward the waiting bus.

"Um, thanks," I said faintly to his retreating back.

———

SUFFICE TO SAY, we all got charged up. The unexpected part was that it wasn't just one type of charge.

No, our EM friends and colleagues became our EM *allies* as soon as Percival explained that Torden was experimenting on Stickmen in the south yard. *That* did not sit well with anyone — Walter excluded; he was neutral, having apparently already known about it. As for the others, they were outraged. After a lifetime of being told to avoid Stickmen at all costs, their supposed leader had one within a few hundred yards of where they slept.

And we hadn't even told them about the pit yet, or the Mega Golem.

So over the course of several hours, we got charged up, big time. Sure, I think we could all take more, EMs can always take more. But we felt sated. Full. Like after a big meal, you know maybe you can have the dessert, but your belly is telling you everything is just fine already.

Ten EMs, full of electricity, pissed off and charged up — with power and with a desire to do something about it.

The dividing wall lowers, and Reggie looks at us via his rearview mirror. "Ms. Hopkins, you want me to turn around. The storm's heading off, but if I take 81 toward Syracuse, you might get another pocket or two."

I scan the others' faces, seeing Percival smile and mouth *We're good*. Hayden and several of the others nod. "Thanks, Reggie. I think we can head home now," I say giving him a smile. If only every regular was so useful and accommodating. Wordlessly, Reggie nods, and the screen goes back up.

Hayden speaks up. "We need to go to the pavilion. Now. We need to confront Torden about this insane experimentation on Stickmen. The idea he has one of those things *near* is terrifying."

"I agree," Mary Kate says. "Come with us. The ten of us can tell the others. Not everyone is in this with Torden. I can tell you that. Most people live at the pavilion because they have nowhere else to go." This I know to be true. Most EMs feel distinctly cast out from society. "I've seen him with his inner circle — we outnumber them."

Zeb and Uma nod, looking determined. "We've got to stop this before someone gets hurt," Zeb says.

Percival, Zee, and I share glances. It's time to rip off the bandage. "Well, there's a bit more to the story," I say.

"More?" Uma says in shock. "More than keeping a Stickman feet from our doorstep?"

"A lot more," Zee says.

"I already knew about the experiments," Walter admits to the others. "Maybe it's because I'm older; they told me. But if there's more, I want to hear it, because I don't really trust any of it. What else is Torden up to?" Walter looks serious and sober, despite the high of getting a charge. He's really interested in this information. "Why haven't you told us the full story already?"

I clear my throat. "Because, frankly, we didn't know if we could trust you all completely. No offense, but we've been banned, and we didn't know truly who was on what side. But now, given what you want to do — go back and confront him about a single Stickman — you need to know the full truth. That might be asking for trouble."

"And what's that?" Uma says.

I dip my chin and look upward at them all with a deep seriousness, one at a time. "Torden doesn't just have *one* Stickman, he has many. Maybe hundreds. It was dark, and hard to see, and certainly I didn't take a head count, but it was *a lot*."

Uma shrieks so loud that Reggie pulls the bus off the road and quickly lowers the screen to ask if everyone is all right. I try to convince him we are, but he's a pro, like I said. He sees the blood drained out of the faces of most of his passengers and he's suspicious. But, also like a pro, he can see no one is physically hurt. The screen goes back up and we're back on the road.

"And one more thing. There's something else that Torden is keeping there." You won't be surprised to learn that Uma's second scream is harder to explain to our wonderful and concerned driver, Reggie, but in time I manage it.

When we finally cross the Hudson on the Tappan Zee Bridge, we're too far north to see any of the downtown city lights. We're not going that way, anyway. Co-op City is our destination, where we'll leave our driver friend Reggie behind and make our way to Torden's pavilion.

I wish I could see the skyline of lower Manhattan, because — despite the palpable energy of the nine other EMs in the limo bus — I have a bad feeling about confronting a man crazy enough to run a Stickman zoo.

28

REVELATIONS

The long drive gives us time to come up with a sort of plan, and as nuts as it is, it's better than nothing.

We have to try to protect ourselves, and the others, before we go bounding into Torden's den. And that means doing something about the pit of Stickmen and their buddy, the Mega Golem.

"Does anyone know how strong a Stickman is?" Hayden asks. "Or for that matter, how strong a hundred of them are together? Or for that matter, how strong that giant Stickman thing is?"

Heads shake. *Now what?* I think.

"Why?" Percival asks. "It doesn't much matter how strong they are if a single touch will do us in."

"It matters if we want to trap them in that building," Hayden replies. "I was thinking we could bolt a cap on it, or weld something over it."

Walter scoffs, dropping his phone to his lap. He had been idly tapping it like a teenage girl. I didn't know whether to be impressed at his youthfulness or sad at how the device sucked him in. "Either of those would be loud and would take a long time. While we're busy trying to do all that, they could just come out and kill us. It would need to be fast, unexpected."

"We need to take out the guard, too," Percival adds.

"How many?" Walter asks.

"Just one, that we saw."

Zeb laughs. "Easy, got it. Leave that to me. Done it a thousand times."

His sister, Uma, slowly turns to look at him, incredulous. "When?"

Zeb smiles. "FPS games. Stealth mode."

Her eyebrows raise dramatically, in a way that tells the rest of us that this is a sibling thing. We should give them a minute and not interrupt. "You sitting on your ass in front of a TV playing games makes you think you can take out a real guard in real life?"

"Yes," Zeb says, still all smiles. "Definitely. And really. I can sneak up, throw something to distract him to look the other way, then wrap him in a headlock. Out cold in under four seconds." All of us are wide-eyed. Then Zeb laughs. "This isn't just from video games, guys! I trained in jiu-jitsu for a few years. A choke out is pretty basic."

Percival gives Zeb a respectful nod. "Okay, then, you're in charge of the guard. We take him down first, then make sure the door is secure. Then, how do we cap the skylight?"

Mary Tate slaps at the wall of the limo bus. "With this," she says, and all of us are confused. "We drop this bus on top of it and seal it up. This thing weighs thousands of pounds."

I wince. "But, my brother and the car service might not appreciate that."

"It's a good idea," Walter adds. *Oh no, they're going to overrule me. Kevin will hate this*, I think. "Just not *this* bus," Walter says. *Good. Thank you, Walter.* "A city bus is better. Bigger and heavier. Over 20,000 pounds, I think."

Zee and Percival's eyes light up. "I don't think even a hundred Stickmen and a Mega Golem could lift that," Percival says, grinning.

"But can we? Can we do it?" Uma asks. "Can we lift such a thing so far and without being caught before the job is done?"

"There, I have some good news," Percival replies. "My particular line of work — which I will not discuss — often forces me into some, shall we say, *challenging* scenarios. Pretty sure that if we find a bus, I can get it running, and steal it."

I turn to him and just stare, which he returns with a perfect white-toothed smile and a toss of his blond curls. My heart wants to flutter, but that's some flighty, stereotypical crap. Instead, I control my emotions and play it all off. "Then what?"

"There are public roads, all the way to the pavilion. We don't have to get crazy and use our EM abilities to float a bus across town. We can drive it most of the way, then a few of us together — maybe three? Me, Walter, and Mary Tate, perhaps? We can lift it, and drop it down on that skylight before anyone's the wiser. Once Zeb tells us the guard is down, that is."

"Roger," Zeb says, winking, and I have a minor panic attack that this whole operation is more amusing than serious for the boys.

"I want to be the one to confront Torden," I say, in a strong voice to try to bring us back to our real goal, and how important it is.

"And me," Zee says, her voice trembling. She's thinking about Robin. I put a hand on her hand, silently.

"Me, too," Hayden interjects, before sheepishly adding, "especially since you two are technically banned and someone else will have to get you inside." He taps his chest with a thumb.

"Okay, then it's set, with only a couple of tweaks," Percival says, clearly enjoying the conspiratorial nature of the work we're about to undertake far too much. "Walter, Mary Tate, and I get the bus and get into position. Zeb tackles the guard below. Uma, do you want to go with your brother and help as a lookout?" She nods. "Okay. Once that's done, we seal the skylight with the bus. Then, Hayden, you take Lyn, Zee, and the rest in to confront Torden and expose him to the others inside. Assuming all our jobs are done, we'll all meet you inside. And of course, everyone talks *our* way. No speaking aloud."

"Of course," Walter says, and the others — myself included — nod in unison. For an old guy, Walter looks especially excited about what we're going to do.

And with that, we're ready. Holy crap. We're taking part in a coup d'état. It's not exactly how I saw my day playing out.

———

I WON'T BORE you by telling you everything all over again. Everything we said we were going to do, we did. It went perfectly. Sure enough, Zeb can choke out a guard; sure enough, Percival can steal a bus. Still amazed at what we've done, I walk into the court of Torden, our false king, grinning ear to ear. It was time for him to get what was coming. Hayden even managed to quickly drum up support, so we have a couple dozen EMs standing in a ring around Torden's little throne in his candle-lit throne room. "Give it up, Torden. All this insanity with experiments and Stickmen in the south wing is done now," I say. I glance over at Zee, and we're a little smug with our obvious victory.

"Dear Lyn," Torden says, sitting calmly, with a low laugh. Beside him, Rand echoes his laughter, giving me a really bad feeling. The same really bad feeling I had before we started, before things went so seemingly well. "Why am I not surprised to see you? Though I suppose I should be more disappointed in the others with you, for letting you in and violating my decree." He gives Hayden in particular a noticeably vicious grin. You might be surprised how quickly the devil comes out in a two-hundred-year-old man's face when he's giving a vicious grin. On second thought, that might not be surprising at all. "Never mind. Lyn — do you know anything about investments? Your family has wealth, and you live in the city with the largest stock exchange in the world." I just stare, not understanding why Torden is asking such strange questions. "Let me give you some words of advice from the investment world. *Don't put all your eggs in one basket.*"

"What are you talking about?" I ask.

"Did you think the only things to worry about were in the south wing?"

Once more, Torden and Rand laugh.

29

STRENGTH IN NUMBERS

We are, quite suddenly, in very deep shit.

Instinctively, Zee and I pull back, but our friends — Hayden, Karen, and Bobby from our storm chasing brigade, and the others they managed to pull in from the pavilion — are used to Torden. They don't distrust him as completely as I do.

More specifically, they don't have the sense to fear him. Not yet, at least.

That changes in an instant, as some of Torden's EM cronies quickly grab both Karen and Bobby. Hayden pulls away, but then we all stop. We're not going to just let Torden have his way with our friends.

Still, he sits there all smug, with Rand whispering something in his ear. They smile at each other in a satisfied way. I find myself truly hopeful I can one day smack that look off both of their faces. Today would be a great day to do it.

But things get worse fast. Torden idly raises one index finger and a door opens behind the throne that I had no idea was even there. Was it a coincidence? So close behind him? I think no, but would others see it the same way?

Standing in the doorway, completely still — one of the most

bizarre and alien things I've ever seen — is a Stickman. Beside me, Zee gasps and tears flow. It's Robin. Despite being bones wrapped in a burned husk of charred skin, we're sure of it.

For a moment, all is still. I don't even hear anyone breathing. Then Torden points and Robin the Stickman lurches ahead with an unbelievable speed. The same kind of leaping, dodging, feral speed we saw at the Fuse Box, but now in an even smaller space.

I only have time to gasp and stagger backward before the Stickman — my friend Robin — pounces on my friend Hayden, pinning him down. With something like glee, it sucks the electricity from Hayden, and we see Hayden quickly start to be burned alive with his own power — the power we all so recently refilled.

I raise my hand in anger and defiance, about to fire an arc of blue energy at the monster, then stop myself, unsure. *Robin! Please stop, Robin!* But it's no use. I shake my head, reminding myself that the real Robin is gone. "I'm sorry," I say to Robin, to Zee, to myself, a millisecond before sucking in all of my electromagic power and blasting it in a devastating lightning bolt of force, hitting the Stickman Robin directly in the gut. The attack is enough to pull Robin up from his prey, but not enough to blast him off like I hoped. Instead, they are a contrast of poses — Hayden limp on the floor, and Stickman Robin taut and electrified above him. I keep feeding my power into him, praying for the moment Torden told me should be possible — when the circuit would break — but nothing happens. We're stuck in sort of hideous trance where I keep firing and the Robin Stickman keeps sponging up my power.

I'm going to fail.

I know it.

I've felt my power drain for many years now. I know what it's like when I've used it all and need a recharge, need to find some willing storm to fill me back up. I feel that drain now, happening quickly. This Stickman will take everything I have and then I'll be powerless. And then, when he's done with Hayden, he'll come for me.

Still firing a massive bolt of electricity, seeing it arc blindingly between my hands and the foe who was once my friend, I scan the room, wondering if it's the last thing I will ever see. Torden, sitting on his stupid throne, has his eyes closed like he's in rapture. Sadistic bastard. But Zee. Seeing her breaks my heart. She's watching what I'm doing, knowing I'm doing it to Robin, and yet knowing it isn't Robin anymore.

Suddenly I know what we have to do.

"Zee," I say through clenched teeth. "Help me. Please."

Zee is frozen, still staring at the Stickman Robin, a charred horror, shivering with the consumption of electricity.

"Zee, please. I'm running out. I need you."

Still nothing.

"Robin," I say.

Zee turns.

"Help me give Robin peace."

And then, wiping her tears away fiercely, Zee fires her own EM power into the Stickman, making such a brightness in the room that it seems the sun itself has come into these four walls. A second goes by and Stickman Robin keeps sucking up the energy like he'll never stop. Until, finally, he does.

There is a sickening pop as Stickman Robin is blasted off Hayden like he's strapped to a rocket, slamming into the far wall and falling into a puddle of limbs. He doesn't move again, his body smoldering such that it fills the room with a dark smoke and foul odor. It's an acrid, almost metallic-smelling stench that feels like it clings to the vessels in my nose, throat, and lungs and might never leave me again.

I stagger.

I'm reeling and I might fall.

No, I can't. There's still Torden and his Clan of Assholes. Yes, even in my stupor I think that name. But Torden looks like someone has cold-cocked him, maybe knocked him out. Rand hovers over him with worry. Between that and the smoke, there's enough confusion that I decide we need to make a break for it. Grabbing Zee's arm I utter a harsh whisper. "Run!"

———

TORDEN'S PAVILION is a maze of rooms, some lit and refurbished — communal spaces or bedrooms for EMs living here; we avoid those — and others dark, dank, and bordering on what should be condemned. Zee and I pant as we run for our lives into those dark places, and a cloying, unpleasantly wet and musty smell seeps into my lungs, blending with the sharp odor from killing a Stickman. My body keeps forcing me to suck in air, but my mind wants nothing more than to push it all out. It all smells like poison. As we run down dark hallways, I see blotches of dark mold that creep up the walls like Rorschach tests. *This one looks like a butterfly*, I think, knowing such thoughts are usually what gets me into more trouble, not out. *Stop it. Focus.* "We need to find a way out, get back to the others!" I shout at Zee as we turn a corner, somewhere in the bowels of the pavilion.

"Lyn... What if they've been captured?" Zee says. "Or worse."

No, I'm not going to think like that. Percival is out there. I shake the thought out of my head and keep on, searching. Finally, we enter a large, tall space. The ceiling is too high to see in such low light, but ahead, we can make out a door. Cautiously, we approach it.

"Do you think it leads outside?" Zee asks.

I reach for the knob. "One way to find out."

Just before my fingertips brush the smooth, round metal of the knob, I hear it. Scratching on the other side of the door.

"Is that —?" Zee starts before I shush her with a harsh whisper. Slowly, quietly, we back away from the door. The scratching increases, and then, startling us both, something pounds on the door with force. *It is a Stickman, and it wants to come in.* I remember from the encounter in my bedroom that Stickmen can smell us when we're too close, and that makes me wonder why none of the ones at the pavilion had done so until now, especially with so many EMs around. You'd think their Stickman noses would be overflowing with the smell of us all. The reason immediately becomes clear to me. "Torden doesn't just *keep* these Stickmen, Zee. He *controls* them. That's why they don't overrun the pavilion. That's why we were able to get so close to them in the south wing without being attacked. He makes them docile here."

There's another loud bang from the other side of the door. "This one doesn't seem so docile now!" she says.

"No, of course not. Torden's got his dogs hunting now." I wonder what that means for Percival and the others, as well as the rest of the EMs. In the confrontation, I couldn't even see clearly what happened to Hayden, or Karen, or Bobby. Hell of a friend I am.

I start to turn around, to lead us away from the door and its waiting Stickman, when I hear another sound from the direction we came.

Torden, in a deep, booming voice, barks commands. "There she is. There's the so-called *Lightning* Hopkins. Kill her and give me her power."

30

THE ANGER QUOTIENT, REVISITED

T he damn thing is taller than I thought. I really hadn't seen it all that well in the dark of the pit. Worse, it was way, *way* uglier.

Torden stands before us, almost gloating, but mostly just, I don't know. Confident? Yeah, probably that. Because behind him is the hulking mass of the thing I called the Mega Golem. It's 12 feet tall, maybe more, and up close and personal, the monstrosity of its cobbled-together head is a thing of nightmares. Well, fine, it had already given me a nightmare. It was a thing of *more* nightmares.

The charred heads of six Stickmen stare at us with their blackened eye sockets of horror. So close, I realize the parts — head, arms, legs, torso — aren't *tied* together, they're *woven*, in a way that their very flesh seems to be melting into each other. Or maybe in the way that, after a house fire, it's hard to tell the ceiling joists from the wall studs from the stair rail. They're all just lumps of ash, all tossed together. My stomach roils. But I can't show fear, not now. Not to this son of a bitch. "Nice pet. What do you call it?"

Momentarily, Torden looks confused, which gives me a perverse happiness. "Call it?"

"You made that thing, right?"

"Yes," he says with pride.

"And you didn't give it a name?"

Torden scoffs. "What does it matter? Call it what you like, because it will be your doom."

"All right, then. Have it your way." I am really ticked off, and when that happens, I usually say shit I might regret. Today's no different. "I'm gonna call him *Tony*, because how could anything named Tony hurt a fly?" I wave, insanely. "Hi Tony!"

Torden makes a disgusted, animal grunt. "Enough of this nonsense." He gestures toward us, and the Mega Golem Tony starts for us.

There's no escape. Torden and his pet thing block the way we came in, and the door behind us is still being scratched and pounded on by some overly zealous Stickman on the other side. So I do the one and only thing I can think of.

As my electromagic power bubbles to the surface, I roll my head around in a circle, hearing little pops in my neck. My hair begins to rise from the electricity flowing through me, so I pull up my hoodie with one hand, seeing little arcs of blue jump between my fingers. Then, I yell and blast the Mega Golem with as much power as I can, hoping to pop its circuits and put it out of my misery, same as I'd done — with Zee's help — to the Stickman Robin.

Immediately, it feels futile. I'd used so much energy on Robin that the well feels not quite dry but awfully damn far from full. Doing some mental math, I figure that if it took most of my strength, plus some of Zee's, to take out one Stickman, I have no chance of taking out a creature composed of multiple Stickmen meshed together. But there's literally nothing else to do — no way out, no other hope. I keep yelling, keep blasting the creature, dead center. It has the effect of stopping the Mega Golem from moving forward, which is nice, but all it really seems to be doing is sucking up what little power I have left.

To one side, Torden holds his arms slightly away from his body on each side, head titled back, eyes closed. Again with the rapturous posture. Why?

Though I keep firing at the Mega Golem, I stop yelling and suck air in through my teeth, the horrible revelation of truth suddenly apparent. Torden had said *kill her and give me her power.* That's what he has these things for. "Zee, the Stickmen — even this one — they take our power, and they *give it to Torden.*"

Beside me, Zee jolts with the shock of realization. It means the worst thing possible. Torden sent the Stickman to the Fuse Box. Torden was the reason it sucked up Robin's life, and now, the very essence of Robin is inside this two-hundred year old demon of a man. It's appalling. Disgusting. Zee screams, a high-pitched, awful scream, as she fills herself with power and shoots blue arcing electricity into the belly of Torden himself.

He stiffens, and for a moment I almost allow myself to think Zee has hurt him. But I know all too well what it means for an EM to attack an EM with power. We all use the same electricity. It's like one battery charging another, while depleting itself. Pointless. Torden shakes his head, looking down his nose at Zee like she is a helpless, petulant child.

"Zee, stop!" I say, still shooting my own blue lightning into the Mega Golem. "Zee — you're just giving him your energy!"

She screams and screams and I think she's never going to stop, until she finally does, cutting off the electric bolts of force. Then Zee's shoulders fall. She looks defeated, deflated. I know that in short order, I will be, too. My reserves are nearly gone.

Across the room, Torden laughs. "You *both* are giving me your power. Thank you," he says. "Because you're right, Lyn. These creatures — the Stickman, and this larger variety I've crafted myself — they are conduits with one purpose. To take *your* electromagic power and to give it to *me.*"

I grimace, not wanting to shoot any more energy into the Mega Golem, but knowing if I don't it will just attack, and it's touch will bleed me dry anyway. A complete catch-22. I'm literally damned if I do, and damned if I don't. Torden once more closes his eyes, feeling the joy of power — my power — streaming into him. *Damn it!*

With all the anger and force I can muster, I figure if he wants it from me, he can choke on it. I'll send so much power into the beast so fast that Torden will drown with his own success. My whole life, I've always used EM power with limits — hiding from regulars, using just enough so that I don't tap myself out — but now that's all done. Because this is it. If I don't blast the Mega Golem, it will just sponge up my power. I have to at least try.

I scream, echoing Zee from moments before, and my arcs of power triple in diameter. They aren't trifling lightning bolts of energy, they're wide tunnels of electricity, boring through the air. The giant creature in front of me staggers backward, and that eggs me to throw even more into the attack. No limits, no reserves. If I fail in 30 minutes or 30 seconds, it doesn't matter, because failure is failure. There is only one way out.

I think of the phrase *failure is not an option*. What a load of crap. Failure is *always* an option. Somewhat by design, failure is the ever-present second option after success. And as my unrelenting, unchecked power batters the Mega Golem, I know it to be true. Failure is an option. And it will be mine.

Because the end of the well was in sight. Only a little bit more, and my EM power will be completely used up, with no magical, suddenly-appearing thunderstorm in this dark basement to recharge my empty batteries.

"I'm spent, Zee," I say, not even looking at her.

"No," she says, and fires her own unchecked power at the thing before us, too. "No, please." The thing, the Mega Golem, senses or feels the weakening of my attack and starts to lean in, lean toward me. "No!" Zee comes toward me, despite every instinct to get away from the creature closing in on me.

"Zee, don't — please," I beg. The thing's outstretched collection of many woven-together hands reaches for me, and I wonder about the pointlessness of it all. *If it touches me, I give it all my power. If I fire at it, I give it all my power.* "You've got be running low, too, Zee. If you run out —"

Still sending bolts of energy into the Mega Golem, Zee slides closer, just next to me. "Then we'll end here together." And with that,

Zee puts one arm around me. We both continue to shoot bolts of electricity into the monstrosity before us, but, instantly, something changes.

I've never been connected to another EM while using my power before. If it was weird to be struck by lightning in the arms of Percival, when we both got a charge at the same time atop the Garret Mountain tower, this was even more revolutionary. It was like I suddenly had a *second* well of EM energy, at my fingertips.

"What are you doing?" Torden barks from across the room, feeling the importance of what has accidentally happened. That makes me smile despite the fact that the Mega Golem's fingertips are inches from me. "Stop that!" Torden cries.

I feel the power. Not of one, but of two. A power I've never felt before. EMs are told from the moment they realize their capabilities that they should shun other EMs when it comes to power. Sure, we pair up for relationships and such, and I'm sure others have done like Percival and me, consuming lightning as one. But any *use* of power with another was considered taboo, a drain. If you did it, you lost power and the other EM gained it. But now I see something deeper, better, stronger. If we join together, we can be more. Even greater, I feel like I *understand* Zee more, in this instant. The moment where she and I are both blasting our EM power together. She feels worried, and immediately I sense that she thinks she's tapped out, empty of power. I have such a different opinion. Her well seems so *full* to me, so ready with renewed power. Can she not see that? But wait — that's the problem. Despite the fact that I want nothing more in this moment than to see Torden dead, I have to acknowledge that he was right. My *Quotient*. I can take the same amount of power as another EM and make it last longer. That's why Zee feels empty, and I feel suddenly so very full and ready. I take in a breath, standing tall in front of both the Mega Golem and the pathetic form of Torden. "Don't tell me what to do, old man," I say, spitting anger through a vicious smile. "You and your *thing* are going straight to hell." And then I tap Zee's power, combining our strength into something more...

A wall of white-blue force slams into the Mega Golem, and we're blinded by the explosion it causes. Zee and I both are blown off of our feet.

Our ears ring and our eyes tear as we release our combined powers. We rise to a seated position, looking at the room through a blur. Slowly, the blinding brightness subsides, and once more we can see the large room before us in all its disheveled glory.

The Mega Golem is dead, burned through like a blown circuit, its various knit-together parts strewn like litter on a windswept side street. Small arcs of blue electricity still course up and down the individual parts at random, sailors trying to find a port, or the weary seeking shelter for the night.

And Torden is gone.

I listen, probably for too long, then jump to my feet. At the door, I don't hesitate, turning the knob and yanking it open. If there's a Stickman on the other side, he's gonna pay.

But there's nothing, and now all I can think is that Percival is out there, with a hundred or more other Stickmen.

I step through the open door, but turn back for a moment, toward my friend. Mackenzie is slower to understand what's happened, and the importance of what it means, but she'll get there soon. Of that, I have no doubt. "Come on, Zee," I say. "It's time we thinned the herd."

31

A FRIEND IN NEED

O utside, the world is in chaos.

Well, I think it is. As soon as we step out the door, we're attacked. A lone Stickman dashes in from the left, and we literally roll on the ground to avoid being touched. We're both tired, we both feel nearly tapped out. Running is essentially our only option.

I want to fight, not because it's a smart idea, but because I'm pissed off and when you're pissed off you're likely to make bad decisions. I raise my hand to fire at the Stickman, only to find another hand on mine. Zee's.

"No," she says. "You can't do everything. We need to run."

"I need to kill this thing," I say.

Zee's eyes are locked on mine. "And what if Percival dies while you do this? Will you be able to forgive yourself?"

I shake my head in anger. "We have no idea what Percival is doing now, or where he is."

"Right," Zee says, her eyes welling with tears that make me think of Robin. Shit, *she's* thinking of Robin. "Isn't the most important thing right now to find the people we love?" *Love?* I think. *Love? Is it that, really?* But I know one thing for certain. Love or not, if this night ends and Percival dies, I will die. That I truly believe.

It's a liberating feeling, honestly. Because now, I will do anything... *anything*... to stop these damned Stickmen. Not just one of them, but all of them. I'll do anything to make sure Percival is safe.

Even if it kills me.

WE RUN, but of course the Stickman we encountered follows, dashing in its feral way, skittering left and right. Meanwhile, we make as straight a line as possible, across the curving open courtyard on the beach side of the pavilion, heading for the south wing. Though it's dark, I see a faint blue glow up ahead, toward the beach, and that makes me run even faster. Which is why I nearly run over a friend in the dark. Nearly, but not quite. "Zeb?"

He doesn't reply, but instead makes an animal hissing sound, way too close to my right ear.

"Lyn!" Zee shouts from behind. "Look out!"

I have a moment to feel sorrow. *Zeb, no, really?* Suddenly, a burst of electromagic zaps through the space between us, and we both stagger away from it and each other. Zee has the sense to try to separate us before the Stickman Zeb has time to touch me. That's how close I come to losing my life for no good reason. I make a mental note to thank Zee if I ever get the chance, and then I roll away and up, turning back to add a bolt of my own. Stickman Zeb dodges both attacks. Behind Zee, the original Stickman is rapidly approaching. "We need to get out of here!" I shout, looking around frantically. *Up,* I think. *If we could get to the roof, it will at least take them a minute to scramble up.* Plus, I need to see if Percival is there. He has to be there. "Zee — follow me!" Then I glow with power and leap into the air, flying in a short arc to the rooftop of the south wing.

There's no one there.

Worse, the city bus used to cap the skylight has been knocked aside, and the dark hole leading to the interior of the building sits like a gaping wound.

A blue glow drops in next to me: Zee. We share a confused look. An instant later, those looks change to grave concern as two other blue glows arc toward us — one from atop the pavilion, one from the beach. Walter lands first, followed quickly by Uma. I let go of the breath I didn't realize I had been holding, glad to see friends and not enemies. But Uma... does she know about Zeb? One look at the redness of her eyes tells me she does. *Damn it.* "What happened out here?" I ask, trying really hard to avoid making it sound like an accusation.

Walter looks at his feet in shame. "The big thing you told us about — it broke out. Pushed the bus off the skylight like it was a toy. Now it's out there somewhere."

"No, it's not. It's dead," I say, matter-of-factly.

Walter is stunned. "How?"

I point at Zee. "We killed it. Together. But where are the others? Where's Percival?" *Please please please please don't tell me anything bad*, I think. *He has to still be alive. He can't be one of those things.*

Walter shakes his head and my heart stops beating. All the air leaves my lungs and I feel like I can't breathe. He slowly points to the open skylight. "When the big one got out, Percival told us to find you. Then he went in there to hold back the rest of the Stickmen. Mary Tate went in with him."

In there? *Are you out of your mind, Percival?* "Oh my God," I say, rushing to the edge of the hole and peering down into total darkness. *Show me a blue glow down there. Come on.* But there's nothing.

"Zeb, no..." Uma whimpers behind me. "Please come back." I turn and see the Stickman Zeb scramble over the half-wall and onto the roof, immediately followed by the other that had been chasing us.

"Come on!" Walter shouts, turning away, ready to blast into the sky and be gone.

"Wait!" I say. "Trust me for a minute, please." Without thinking, the four of us quickly form a sort of defensive semi-circle, Uma on my left. I turn to her. "Please trust me, Uma. We can set Zeb free."

Uma's tears are streaming, watching the approaching form of her ruined brother as a Stickman. "What do I need to do?" she asks through a clenched jaw.

"Just take my hand," I say. "All of us, at the same time."

"What good will that do?" Walter says, nearly frantic. "Just sap all out power, right when we need it most. We need to go!"

"No, please, just for a minute. Please." I hold out my hands, and Zee takes my right. After a moment, Uma takes my left. Zee reaches for Walter's hand, and, though he looks bewildered and unconvinced, he grabs it. "Okay, now. All together. Uma and I will fire at Zeb, so we can release him. You two get the other one. On three..." The creatures close in and I feel the trembling of Uma's hand. "One... Two... *Three!*"

Two plus two should equal four, but with my Quotient, there's a strange multiplication going on, too. Blasts of electromagic hit the two Stickmen, filling them with light and energy. "Push hard! Now!" I scream, and we all force energy into the bolts. The Stickmen pulse and glow, then simultaneously flash with a brilliance as their circuits pop and they fall. The charred and lifeless husks of Zeb and the other drop to the rooftop, still.

Slowly, we let go of each other's hands. Beside me, Uma cries and I hear her whisper, "Goodbye, brother."

Goodbye, I think, cursing the word. *I'm not saying that word again. Not now. Not tonight.* I move to stand over the open skylight. *Give me something, Percival. Some kind of sign.*

And, like fate, he does. Below me in the pit, I hear the distinct sound of electromagic being fired, zaps and pops. It's faint — not close enough for me to see anything, not even the barest traces of flickering blue — but it's there.

"I'm going down." It's not up for debate.

"Me, too," Zee says, coming up next to me. I give her a smile of thanks. Because, frankly, we've just learned that multiple EMs together are much more powerful, and I'm pretty sure power will be needed once I make this jump.

"I'll go," Walter says. "I can't tell you how many years it's been drilled into my head — into everyone's heads — not to come near another EM when you or they are using power. We were told one will just suck up the power of the other. Now, seeing what we just did together, I feel like I've been tricked for my whole life. And I know who was doing the tricking."

We all do. Torden.

I realize that with Walter joining us, Uma will be left on her own. Not ideal with Stickmen potentially all around, and her just losing her brother. "Uma, it's okay for you to leave. You can go home. Just don't stay here. It isn't safe."

With the back of one hand, she wipes away her tears like they're an insult. "And leave my friends in there? No way. Let's go. Besides, it looks like we have a secret weapon now." She smiles, and before I can argue, Uma steps off the roof and drops into the pit. The rest of us rush to catch up.

———

THE INSIDE of the south wing building is darker than midnight on a moonless night with a towel over your head. That, friends, is a really weird phrase my father used to say. But it's appropriate now. I scoff, quietly and to myself, once more thinking of my father. The person I never knew had EM power.

Lucky for us, our electromagic is like a built-in flashlight. Four blue glows aren't strong enough to see everything in the wide space, but we illuminate enough to know that we're alone.

"Where is everyone?" Walter asks.

"Shhh," I say. "Hold on a second." I wait, listening.

Zap! Pop! On my left. "There! Come on!" I lead the group through a large archway and into a second wide room. On the far wall are several doors, none labeled in any way I can see. So, we were going to play a game — choose the right door and win a prize. Percival's life.

I chose the middle one, jerking it open to find a short hallway leading to a third large space, this one seems to be a wide garage. Tractors and other work vehicles are parked on the sides, though they're hard to see with all the bodies in the way. Stickmen scramble over everything. And in the middle of the space, two faint blue glows tell me the one thing I need to know more than anything else in the world.

Our friends are still alive. Percival is still alive. My heart beats like it's been dug out of a grave and shocked back to life.

But one thing is clear: their energies are waning, down to fumes and hope. Even in so little light, I can see it. Percival looks utterly exhausted, so low that I doubt he could power my dad's old AM radio. How could he not be, trapped in a room with untold numbers of Stickmen, running and dodging and firing for dear life. If we don't do something immediately, Percival and Mary Tate will die.

And that is something I will not permit.

32

WHAT IS IT GOOD FOR?

S creaming like a banshee, I enter the room followed by my friends. "Everyone! Grab hands and fire! Anything that moves that isn't one of us! But keep pushing forward — we have to make it through to them *now*!"

Walter is apparently now a true believer, because he grabs my hand eagerly, before anyone else. Zee and Uma join to each side, and then it's like the goddamned Fourth of July. Zapping bolts of blue-white electricity spray forth from the four of us, stabbing at Stickmen all around the room. Most of our attacks hit Stickmen in the back, considering how we're late to the party.

Not expecting anyone behind them, we're remarkably successful at pinning a few Stickmen in place. The others turn, realizing there is a new enemy. Percival and Mary Tate see us coming in, and I can only assume they're confused as hell seeing four EMs with their arms locked, shooting bolts. But the results can't be dismissed. We have the attention of the Stickmen, though at first they probably think of us as another nuisance at best — another prey at worst.

That all changes when I pulse my energies at one of the Stickmen nearest to Percival, and its circuit blows, dropping it dead on the floor. Suddenly the others freeze.

I smile.

Yep, I smile. I'm stuck in a dark room with untold numbers of Stickmen, and I freakin *smile*. Why? Because we just gave them an *oh shit* moment. That's worth a smile, right?

"Pers! Mary Tate! Grab hands!" I shout. I know they'll be confused. For an EM, it would be like me telling them to stick a fork in a wall outlet and suck up the electricity from it. It can be done, but our whole lives we've been warned against it. At least we know what the results are with wall outlets. We've seen it. But this whole rule not to use power when you're in contact with another EM is something we really didn't spend any time verifying. We just trusted it to be true, because it seemed like it should be. It is amazing to me how this one simple lie has kept EMs apart for so long, but it has. I know they're more than skeptical, but seeing me holding hands with Zee and the others, and considering the desperate spot they're in, they do it.

And then they each fire a tentative burst of electricity.

Immediately, I see their expressions change to surprise. Together, they are stronger. They lean on each other, sharing their Quotient. I still think they're nearly tapped out, but any little extra boost is welcome. We continue to push through, Stickmen scattering to each side as we fire bolts at them, bolts they now realize are deadly.

But they don't fear us. Not yet. They shift and come in from other directions, but they're not giving up. I lock into one on my left and sent an arc of blue power toward it, catching it in the side of the head. Quicker than expected, its circuit pops and it falls. "Try aiming for the head — it may short circuit them faster!"

Zee's first to try it, and sure enough, it works. Of course, it helps that there are so many Stickmen and they are so close to us — that makes aiming for a specific spot easier. In short order, she downs another one. A moment later, Walter does the same.

All the sudden, the feeling in the room changes. The Stickmen stop frantically attacking, and instead begin to back away and circle warily. It's enough of a break that we get to Percival and Mary Tate, who are using a wall to protect their backside. Zee, Walter, and Uma turn around in unison, forming a sort of defensive ring, but I rush straight to Percival, and I punch him, hard.

"Hey, what the heck was that for?" he says. Up close, I see the sweat, the redness of his face. He's exhausted.

"You idiot — are you trying to get yourself killed? I —" I choke up on tears, so happy to be standing next to him again. "What would I do if you died? Did you ever think about that?" I start to punch him again, but then he takes my arms and pulls me in to him. Such a feeling of relief washes over me that I don't initially even bother to think that we're sharing a public display of affection *and* we're in a room full of Stickmen.

"Thanks for coming back for me," Percival says, flipping a blond curl behind one ear and smiling with his perfect white teeth. Then he leans down and kisses me. Inside, the energy that had been feeling depleted suddenly feels like nothing next to the welling up in my heart. If he asked me to, I'd take out every Stickman in the room single-handedly.

But I'd rather do it together.

"Guys, a little help," Zee says. Around the others, the Stickmen have started to approach again, their desire for prey a bit too strong to overcome their fear of absolute death.

"Everyone, together!" I shout, grabbing Percival's hand. He takes Zee's free hand and now we have a chain of six EMs. Time to see what that well of power feels like. I reach in to tap it, and it's hard to believe. Though individually, we might all feel spent, together, we feel full of power. I scan the dark room, picking one of the Stickmen who's gotten too close for comfort. Then I blast the thing right between the eyes. In seconds, it pops. "I think I'm getting the hang of this."

"Less talking, more shooting," Walter says grumpily. "Come on everyone, we need to get out of here!" He aims at a Stickman and misses, but quickly changes his angle and hits a second one. Funneling all our strength, our Quotient, combined, Walter pops another Stickman.

With so much death nearby, I expect the air to smell like burned meat or singed hair, but it doesn't. I think Stickmen are already too far gone, been burnt bad enough already, to still smell that way when their circuits go. Instead, the room fills with that acrid scent, the same smell from when we released Robin, but a hundred times stronger, something that reminds me of the moments just after getting a charge from a lightning bolt.

We fire and fire and fire. Many more Stickmen meet their end before the rest finally get the picture. They aren't winning on this day. They hiss and skitter, but now they're moving away, through the door and gone. A last Stickman looks at us defiantly, but when Walter shoots a pissed off arc of blue that misses the thing by only inches, it too runs out. We're alone.

"Should we chase them?" Uma asks. "Get them all?"

But I hear the weariness in her voice and know that we've done enough for now. "Let them go," I say. "We know how to handle those things now."

Uma drops her hands to her sides, a sign of both relief and exhaustion. Then the tears come again. Around us, the bodies of Stickmen are scattered, and although they each have specific characteristics of the person they once were, they are eerily similar. And look far too much like Uma's brother after we released him. I put my arms around Uma with nothing but love and sympathy, and soon the others do the same. Six EMs gathered as one with all the bitter emotions of both victory and defeat.

33

CHANGING OF THE GUARD

Dawn breaks to the east, making the beach start to glow with color as we exit the south wing and head back to the northern section of the pavilion.

Rounding the building, we walk across the paved courtyard in the middle, a decorative compass rose made of bricks below our feet. At nearly its dead center, facing west, I stop.

Torden stands before us, in the wide expanse of pavement near the main entry road. All around him are EMs. Rand and many more. Nearly everyone I'd ever seen at the pavilion.

"This doesn't look like it's over quite yet," Percival whispers beside me.

"Lyn Hopkins!" Torden shouts, raising one hand like a warning. "The guilty party is before us, now, everyone."

"Guilty?" I laugh, incredulous. "Me? That's an interesting thought."

"What other word would you use?" Torden says, looking to those nearest him to echo his sentiments. "You and your friends have stolen from us, and now you've brought death upon us. You got your friend Robin killed by a... *Stickman* as you call them, and then he became one. Worse, you lured him here to follow you. He attacked and nearly killed some of our own. And others of his kind came after. We have yet to tally the dead." I couldn't believe he was saying all this with a straight face. And I was aghast to see heads nodding next to him. "All this, I lay at your feet, Lyn Hopkins. You are guilty of many crimes on this day, and for those crimes, you will have to pay."

I spit words back at him. "You know what, Torden? I've *never* liked you, but until now I never had a reason. Just something about you I didn't trust. After this, I see it clearly. You aren't just a liar, you're evil. You aren't just deceiving these people, you're using them, and, in the end, I assume you'll kill them like you've killed so many others." I look across the other faces gathered around. Unfamiliar ones look back with scorn — I assume those are Torden's inner circle, his Clan of Assholes. I ignore them. I seek out other faces. Skeptics, people who are confused and unsure. I speak to them. "We never stole anything from you! Why would we? What do we need from *you*? And we found your Stickmen — the one you were experimenting on in the yard. Yeah, maybe some people know about that. The work that you say is for the greater good. But these people don't know about the hoard of over a hundred Stickmen you've been keeping in the south wing!" There are audible gasps. People murmur, asking each other if my words could be true. "I don't think many know about your creation either — the creature you *made* from a half dozen Stickmen tied or sewn or bolted together. Do you? Do any of you know about that?" People are turning toward Torden, looking for a reaction, either a rebuttal or an explanation. For the moment, he gives neither, choosing to keep his smug, calm look, to sway the doubters.

Still, as I've seen so many times before, not everyone is as distrusting of Torden as I am. I see faces in the crowd squinting their eyes at me. Wondering why they should trust my word.

"It's true!" Heads turn, and there, supported by Bobby and Karen, is Hayden. His hair is frazzled and maybe his skin looks a tad darker — like spending too much time in a tanning bed — but he's alive. "It's all true, what she's saying. And one of his Stickmen almost killed me. Except Lyn stopped it. Listen to her!"

Good timing, friend. Because I'm not done.

I clear my throat loudly and the crowd turns back my way. "So the question is *why*? Why would Torden keep Stickmen captive and do experiments on them, try to build a bigger, better Stickman?"

"Oh, this should be quite interesting," Torden says, chuckling to Rand. "Listen to her lies, if you like, everyone. And then we will deliver Lyn Hopkins to justice. You all know me. You all know who you can trust. Who's given you this place, a place only for us? Me. I did that. What has *she* ever given you?"

I ignore him, still looking for the doubters. The ones not sure of what I'm saying, not sure of what he's saying. "Did anyone ever wonder why so many of us are young — teens, twenties, thirties, but not many are older than that? Or wonder how it is that Torden is over 200 years old?" *Wait, Lyn*, I tell myself. *Let that point sink in.* So I do. EMs all around turn their heads, noticing — really noticing — the crowd they're standing in. The very young crowd, with only a couple notable exceptions. *Good. Now they can find out.* "Because Torden uses the Stickmen to recharge himself. When a Stickman takes your power, it *gives it to him!*" That rapturous pose when I was sending my electromagic into the Stickman attacking Hayden, and again when we were firing at the Mega Golem. Both times, Torden was aglow with the pleasure of gaining EM energy. "That's why the Stickmen don't have powers of their own. They don't sponge it up for *themselves*. They suck it up and pass it along to Torden. He admitted all this to me and Zee, and he did it with a smile on his face. So now, who do you trust?"

The murmurs of the crowd turn to full-on shouts. Demands for answers, explanations. Torden and Rand try to shout down the others, try to restore order. His CA people start physically grabbing others, telling them to calm down and think about who they're talking to, the accusations being made.

And in the commotion, I don't notice two things until they converge. Behind me in the courtyard, Walter is on his cellphone, quietly making a call; before me on the street, four cars are approaching. It's the headlights that finally get my attention.

A long, sleek car, all black, slowly motors toward us, followed by three identical others. *Those look a heck of a lot like...* "The car service?" I'm so confused, I say it out loud. Zee and those near me turn their heads, confused. I hadn't called the service to pick me up, and even if I had, why would I need four cars? No. Someone was coming. Someone who appeared to know exactly what they would find at Torden's pavilion. From my left, Walter walks by, tapping his phone to disconnect a call as he walks out to meet the incoming cars.

For his part, Torden looks flustered. The vocal dissent around him dies down for a moment, as heads turn to see the approaching vehicles. No one's quite sure what to make out of it, all things considered. Strictly speaking, the park that houses Torden's pavilion is closed overnight, but the sun is rising, so if we're caught in the park early, it isn't by much. Still, those aren't cop cars coming down the lane. Either way, I have to imagine Torden isn't excited about the prospect of anyone noticing us all there at the same time. That might lead to questions, which might lead to investigations.

But who called the car service? I mean, the service we use isn't exclusive to my family, but the coincidence is pretty great — Hold on! My *family* car service?

I am suddenly dumbstruck with possibilities. Could it be...? "Dad?" No. Impossible. He's been gone for years.

The first car reaches the looping turnaround just before us, and dead in the center of the lane, it stops. After a moment when my heart feels like its in my throat, I see Walter step forward and open the rear passenger door. A man starts to get out. Expensive Italian shoes, a finely-pressed dark suit, hair like... "Dad?" I say aloud again. This is not happening. This is not possible.

But he was an EM, my father. That I learned from Walter, rather accidentally. The same Walter who was now greeting him at the car. Who had put down his phone just moments before, probably because he had made the call. And if my father was an EM, who else would interrupt an EM showdown than another EM?

The man stands up and I gasp. It — wait, no. It's not my father. It's even more mind-boggling than that.

It's my brother, Kevin.

"Kevin?" I sputter. "What are you—?"

Standing tall beside the car, Kevin says in a booming voice, "Torden Detonde. Come forward. This is all over now."

Okaaaaaay, so my brother is here and he knows Torden. I am officially confused.

Murmurs and gasps go up from the crowd, but even more audible is Torden himself. He scoffs. "Come forward? *Come forward*? You forget who I am, Kevin Hopkins. You forget yourself, *boy*," Torden says with a twisted grimace. "Speak respectfully to your elders."

This is getting weirder by the second, and I'm having trouble keeping my chin off the ground. Kevin knows Torden, and Torden knows Kevin? And both my mother *and* father were EMs? So the only logical explanation is... "My brother is an EM." Holy freaking shit. As soon as this is all over, he's got a *lot* of explaining to do. "Why didn't he ever tell me?" Zee hears my words, muttering to myself, and grabs my hand to give it a little squeeze of support.

Kevin steps away from the car and, as if they can sense power, the EM crowd parts, letting him walk directly up to Torden and Rand. "No, Torden, you forget yourself. You forget the Oath of the High Order." Yep, my brother's an EM. He knows about the High Order, and, it seems, way more about it than I do. I don't have a clue what the Oath of the High Order is. With all these revelations, I am officially the least observant person in history. Or completely self-involved. Maybe both? Don't answer that.

The next thing isn't surprising. My mouth takes over for my brain. "This isn't possible. Kevin — why are you here?"

My brother turns to me, momentarily, frustrated. It was clear — believe me, I've seen all his moods and expressions — that he had something important to do and didn't want to be interrupted. "Just wait, Lyn. We can talk after."

I nod but mumble to myself. "You got that right."

Torden isn't giving up. "Turn and go home, Kevin. Go back to your fancy house in your fancy car. We don't need your kind around here."

To my surprise, Kevin turns away and for a moment I think he's acquiescing — that he's going to do just what Torden said and go home. Then he speaks, not to Torden, but to the crowd. "Many years ago, a rift started to form between members of the Order. My parents and I were on one side, while Torden and Rand were on the other. Torden was named to the High Order, but he had a strange interest in Stickmen. An obsession, as we saw it. So my parents decided to split from Torden's authority. Not long after, they disappeared." I don't like the way Kevin is describing this one bit. Was Torden responsible for my parents disappearance? "But some of us, of like mind, stayed behind, to keep an eye on Torden and his actions." Kevin turns to Walter and nods. Walter smiles. *Jesus, I've been blind*, I think.

Torden puffs himself up and interrupts. "That's exactly right — you *chose* to break from the group, and so you have no right or authority to be here. To make... *accusations*." Torden spoke the word like it was poison on his tongue.

My brother seems unaffected by Torden's bile, instead waving a hand toward the line of cars in the curved lane. Doors on the middle two open and four people get out. The first thing I notice about them is that they're all old. Not withered and helpless, though. The grey and wrinkled four approaching each look hale and powerful. I find myself unable to pin down a guess on their ages. *Powerful? They're all EMs.* Two women, two men, each ethnically different. In a place like New York, ethnic diversity isn't exactly a surprise, but somehow this feels different. One of them, a man who appears to be Japanese, holds a small box like it's a religious artifact.

The sight of them seems to weaken Torden's confidence. "What is this? Why are they here?" Beside Torden, Rand takes a step backward. There's fear in his eyes, and they're locked on the small box.

The four newcomers pass through the crowd and array themselves beside my brother. Kevin speaks once more with a booming voice. "By decree of the High Order, witnessed by the four elders beside me, I, Kevin Hopkins, assume the position of High Order, New York City. Torden Detonde, you are hereby stripped of your authority and will be tried by your peers for the crimes of oath-breaking, endangerment of your fellow electromagicians, and murder." Kevin quickly glances my way. "Crimes fully exposed by my sister, Lyn, and her friends." Kevin nods appreciatively toward our group. I blush. What can I say? I'm not good with public compliments. Or social interactions. Or, you know, *people*. "Rand Haldor, you will be tried as an accomplice. Others may be as well. This is the decree of the High Order. *Ubi concordia, ibi victoria.*" Whatever those last words are, they sound important. I make a mental note to ask Kevin what the heck that means. Around my brother, Torden's Clan of Assholes suddenly realizes the shit might hit the fan for them, too. They are decidedly less defiant after this realization.

"It's all lies!" Torden spits, pointing at me. "She's never liked me, just like the rest of her family. She's making this up!"

Kevin is calm. "All of that, we will know for certain in time. Come with us now." The driver of the fourth car hops out and opens the rear doors of his car, ready to welcome Torden and Rand. It's Harry, the driver I've known for so long, who brought me home from my last charge-hunt. That seems like a million years ago. Does Harry even know he's taking Torden and Rand to prison? For that matter, is there really an EM prison somewhere? I genuinely need to start learning more about these things.

Torden rages. "I won't go. Kevin Hopkins, this is *my place!* These are *my people!*" Beside him, the others are starting to distance themselves. Not so sure he has people anymore. Even Rand has backed away.

"You took an oath," Kevin says gravely. "And in that oath, you promised to submit yourself to fair trial when and if needed by the other elders for reasonable cause. That time has come. If you do not keep this oath..." The Japanese elder next to my brother opens the small box, and inside I see a smooth, dark orb resting on red velvet. "...you shall be subject to the Touchstone of Mount Hachiro. These are your only options. Come, Torden. Choose sensibly. There is no need for you to touch the stone today. Stand trial. If you are free of guilt, it will be proven."

"My *only options?*" Torden grumbles. "No, *Kevin.* There's another. A third option. Where you can go straight to hell!" Suddenly, Torden is full of blue-white glowing power, a brilliantly bright light I've never seen him wield before, not to this level. I have a millisecond to think he's going to strike at my brother, but that old rule has to stay true, right? Shooting your EM power into another EM is just going to fill them up. That part hasn't changed. I hope.

A look of hatred on his face, Torden glances upward and there is a whooshing rush of power as he shoots himself into the sky. We all stare as he arcs through the air like a rocket taking flight, launching itself to some distant world. I have no idea what world Torden will find out there. If the High Order runs the community of electromagicians, will there be any shelter for him, or will he become a recluse, a hermit? Flying north, high and bright in the morning sun, Torden Detonde disappears from view.

As we're watching, I hear someone mutter, "Well, shit." It's Rand. Clearly hesitant, Rand shakes his head, looks across the faces of the elders in front of him, before his eyes once more come to rest on the box and its dark orb. The sight must settle something in his mind, because, echoing Torden, Rand fills himself with power and bolts into the sky, following his master.

Collectively, all of the gathered EMs — the young ones like me, not the elders who seem reserved and confident — begin to look around, wondering what to do next.

Back at the fourth car, I notice the driver, Harry. His mouth is hanging open, head tilted up to follow the disappearing glow of two people who — in his regular mind — inexplicably just flew away. He stays that way for a moment, then wills himself to shut his mouth and stand up straight. He closes the back doors and then hops back in the driver's seat.

I told you those guys are pros.

34

THE LONGEST ROAD

With only a glance — a magic that isn't magic at all but really just the familiarity of siblings — Kevin urges me to follow him. He walks away from the slowly dispersing crowd, across the courtyard with its inlaid compass rose, and toward the beach. We stroll at a leisurely pace along the curving walkway that separates sand from grass. "How are you holding up, Lyn?"

I don't know where to begin. "Why didn't you tell me? About you? About Dad? And all this time, you've known about me, and Mom? How could I be so blind?"

"You really don't remember?" he asks.

"*Remember*? No, I never knew you and Dad were EMs."

"You did. A *long* time ago," Kevin says. "But you took it hard, finding out how different you were from regular people. You didn't want to accept it, and you drew in to yourself. You didn't want to talk to any of us, ever. Mom eventually cracked through your shell a little bit, which is maybe why you remember what she was. For Dad and me, you never came out of that shell. Even nowadays, how often do you talk to me? Really?"

I didn't answer. I probably blushed. He was right. "Kevin, look.

You and I are very different. The whole wealth thing — huge house, car service, money for everything — that suits you. For me, it feels like I'm cheating. Like I'm living someone else's life. But I want to live *my* life. I can't pretend to be something I'm not." I immediately realize the stupidity of my statement. Weren't we both — and all EMs — always pretending to be something we're not?

Kevin, thankfully, lets that go. "Lyn, if you ever thought I was too forceful with you, trying to get you to be a certain way, act a certain way, then I'm sorry."

I tilt my head to one side and smirk. "Sure, at home. But now it looks like you're the head of all the EMs in the city. Is that right? You're this... *High Order?*"

"Yes, the elders just raised me to that level, joining them."

"But... don't you have to be a lot older or something? You're not an *elder.*"

Kevin laughs. "I'm older than you."

"You know what I mean."

"Of course. But being in the High Order isn't about age, it's about unity and responsibility. I can teach you more about these things, if you're ready to listen now."

I thought about that. Was I? The real answer was *I don't know.* "But... Mom and Dad. Are they really—?"

"Yes," Kevin says calmly. He's good at being calm. Maybe that's why I never felt like I could relate to him. "They're really gone."

"Did Torden do something to them?"

"I don't know."

"Don't you want to find out?" My question comes out full of frustration and emotion.

Kevin replies, still calm. But with an air of deadly seriousness that gives me newfound respect for him. "Yes. Very, very much. Before, I would have been accusing an elder without proof. Now, thanks to you, Torden has been cast down, and I have been raised up. Now I can find out the truth."

Suddenly, and for no good reason, I remember Mr. Gold Muscle

Car, the guy who tried to kill me back in the corn field. "Do you think Torden had regulars working for him?"

"Why do you ask?" Kevin says. I tell him the story, keeping it short, but with enough details to raise his eyebrows. "That is *definitely* something we'll have to check on as well. Exposing EMs to regulars is against the Oath of the High Order, too. Seems like Torden will have a lot to answer for."

"Wait...," I say, trying to make sense of things. "If Mom and Dad both were EMs, and so are you and me, does Juliet know about us all? Especially if exposing us to regulars is against some oath?"

Kevin shrugs. "To my knowledge, no one has ever had that explicit conversation with Juliet."

"That's a non-answer."

"Perhaps," he says, the corners of his mouth hinting at a smile.

I don't know whether to be mad, embarrassed, impressed, or what. Juliet continues to amaze and confound me. I feel like I've been living in the dark for years, and now, finally, the sun is shining. "But what about the drivers? They just saw quite a show."

"Yes, that's unfortunate," Kevin says. "I had hoped to avoid anything like that in front of them, though I warned them that the individual we were going to meet was a type of scientist and may have unusual technology at his disposal. A half-truth. I will remind them each that our contract stresses discretion."

THE CROWD of EMs that had been in the courtyard retreats back to the pavilion. There, everything is abuzz with activity. "What's going on?" I ask my brother.

"They're packing. It's time to leave this place," Kevin says. "Well, more accurately, it's time for it to be shut down."

"Where will they go?"

The devious grin that dawns on Kevin's face tells me he has something planned. "I have an idea or two about that."

"But the pavilion is done? No more?"

"Yes, we want to make a clean break from Torden's rule. Besides, this whole place is Exhibit A; we need to do a thorough check of everything here. Torden can't run forever, and what we find here will be evidence against him. Thanks to you."

I roll my eyes. I don't like praise. It's embarrassing. "What did I do? You already knew all about Torden."

Kevin stops, giving me an earnest look. "That's not true at all. I suspected Torden's ideology diverged from the High Order, but had nothing firm to go on. Walter lived here and he told us about the experiments Torden was doing on a single Stickman. It was *strange* but it wasn't against our oath. And, Torden said he was trying to do it to better understand a creature that can kill us. We couldn't put him on trial for trying to *help* EMs, right?"

"But how could you — how could Walter — not see the hoard of Stickmen he had here, so close by?"

Kevin smiles. "Lyn, you're not the only one who can sometimes miss the forest for the trees. Torden had accomplices, some of whom are still among us. We'll be talking to everyone. Lots of questions. Those other EMs that knew what he was doing and kept supporting him — we'll sort them out. But those people helped him hide what he was doing. It wasn't until you, Zee, and Percival started snooping around independently that Torden's secrets really started to leak out."

I wave one hand, brushing off the complement. *Percival*, I think. *I need to talk to Percival.* I make some excuse about leaving my brother to the important work of closing down the pavilion, then I head outside.

Eventually, I find Zee chatting with Hayden and a few of the others. Wordlessly, we hug. She's my friend and tomorrow will be another day for us. I ask her if she's seen Percival.

Zee smiles, pointing toward the beach. "He kept all those Stickmen busy while we were under attack," Zee says with a twinkle in her eye. "I guess we're not the only ones who will do anything it takes to protect the ones we love."

There she goes with that love stuff again.

———

"Tired?" I ask Percival, plopping down on the park bench beside him.

"Like you wouldn't believe," he says, smiling his perfect smile. He tosses a curl of blond over one ear, then slides toward me, putting one arm over my shoulders. "You'd think that F5 I got would have kept me going longer, but I don't think I've used this much power in... well, forever."

I lean into him. "This has been a crazy few days," I say, the understatement of the year. "What do we do now?"

I ask the question not trying to be full of portent, speaking about *our* potential future together, but out loud, that's exactly what it sounds like. "I don't know, Lyn. What *do* we do now?"

How should I know? We've set foot on a new road together, and I have no idea where it goes. Rather than answer — rather than say something to ruin a thing I don't even fully understand yet — I just lean into him more, and his arm wraps tighter around me.

We sit like that for some time, watching the sun climb its ladder into the sky.

35

THE MORE THINGS CHANGE

My phone buzzes as Percival and I walk back toward the parking lot, his arm still around my shoulders, my arm around his waist. With my other hand, I dig the phone out of my pocket and give it a quick glance.

Sometimes it's hard to explain why people do things. I can't explain why *I* do things, except to simply say that's what *I* do. That's me being me. I give Percival a little squeeze, then curl out of his embrace to stand face to face with him. "Hey, sorry. Can you give me a minute? I need to take this call."

Percival flashes his blindingly bright smile, unfazed. "Sure, Lyn. No problem. I'll go check to see if Hayden or any of the others needs help." He turns and heads toward the pavilion.

I look back at my phone. There's no incoming phone call. So, yeah. I don't seem to be starting this whole possible serious relationship with Percival thing off on the right foot. Instead, what's on my screen is a red message.

About weather.

Severe Weather Alert: Tomorrow afternoon, a line of violent supercell thunderstorms is predicted to cross eastern South Dakota, beginning near the Missouri River and heading east along I-90. Residents in the area are urged to seek shelter once the system develops, as tornadoes of class F4 or higher are possible. Chance of precipitation: 100%.

Okay, *that* caught my attention. F4. Or higher.

I swipe away from the alert and check a map of the area, then I make a few calls.

Fifteen minutes later, I'm walking alone down the side of City Island Road near that old golf course when a taxi pulls over. "Hey miss — you call a cab?" the driver shouts through the open window. I nod and get in. "Where to?"

"JFK, please," I reply. The driver starts the meter and pulls out. I spare one look out the rear window, knowing that I'm leaving an awful lot behind, but it isn't permanent. I'll be back in a day or two. I know they'll be pissed that I ran off, Percival and Zee in particular, but a girl's got to get her charge when she can. Given everything I've just been through, it's more than just my well of EM power that needs a lift. I'm spent, emotionally and physically. I need a moment.

"Where are ya flying today?" the driver asks, eyes looking back at me in the rearview mirror.

"Sioux Falls," I reply, giving him a broad smile. "I've never been there, and I hear the weather is nice this time of year."

THE END

of

STRUCK

Lightning Hopkins
Book 1

NEWSLETTER

Sign Up for Keith Soares's New Releases Newsletter

Get release news and free books, including private giveaways and preview chapters. To join, just visit KeithSoares.com and select the option at the top of the page to get two free books, or go directly to the newsletter sign up form.

facebook.com/KeithSoaresAuthor
twitter.com/ksoares

ABOUT THE AUTHOR

Keith Soares

For 22 years, Keith Soares ran an interactive game, web, and app development agency working with clients like National Geographic, PBS, Verizon, HarperCollins, and the Smithsonian Institution. As a team leader dealing with agency deadlines and late nights waiting on code updates, he converted some of the inevitable downtime into creative time and started writing science fiction and fantasy novels in 2013.

In 2020, Keith left the agency world behind to become a full-time author, trading computer code for plot outlines. He lives in Alexandria, Virginia, with his wife and two daughters, who are all avid readers.

If you've enjoyed this book, I hope you'll consider leaving a very brief review with the store where you purchased it. Thanks.